Praise for
A Good Place to Leave a Lover

"These stories are a joy to read. I loved the prose full of poetry and the insights on the two cultures—the ways in which they clash and learn from each other—as well as the humor that sparkles through. Gattig shows Japanese and American characters in fresh and original situations, enlightening both sides in the process."

—Minae Mizumura,
author of *Inheritance from Mother*

"I savored this beautiful book. The stories are doors into nuanced worlds, and they will linger in your mind long after you turn the last page. *A Good Place to Leave a Lover* is sensual, subversive, and masterful."

—Pamela Rotner Sakamoto,
author of *Midnight in Broad Daylight: A Japanese American Family Caught Between Two Worlds*

"A tour de force. Like pearls on a string of revelations, these stories show values and grievance on both the American and the Japanese side."

—Jim Nelson, author of *Bridge Daughter*

"These rich, entertaining stories show the complexities of cross-cultural romance, taking the reader on interlapping waves across the Pacific. Filled with longing and cultural searching, the writing often stops you in your tracks with sharp, unexpected insights. Like a pointillist painting, the collection is precise and colorful, leaving a deep impression on the imagination."

—Damian Flanagan, author of *Yukio Mishima*

A Good Place to Leave a Lover
by Nicolas Gattig

© Copyright 2024 Nicolas Gattig

ISBN 979-8-88824-527-9

All rights reserved. No part of this publication may be reproduced, stored in a retrieval system, or transmitted in any form or by any means—electronic, mechanical, photocopy, recording, or any other—except for brief quotations in printed reviews, without the prior written permission of the author.

This is a work of fiction. All the characters in this book are fictitious, and any resemblance to actual persons, living or dead, is purely coincidental. The names, incidents, dialogue, and opinions expressed are products of the author's imagination and are not to be construed as real.

Published by

3705 Shore Drive
Virginia Beach, VA 23455
800-435-4811
www.koehlerbooks.com

A GOOD PLACE TO LEAVE A LOVER

NICOLAS GATTIG

VIRGINIA BEACH
CAPE CHARLES

Some of the stories in this collection have been previously published in *Asia Literary Review, Eastlit, 34th Parallel, The Font,* and *New Feathers Anthology.*

For Mai Masaki

CONTENTS

A Good Place to Leave a Lover

A Human Accident

The Android Rebellion

A Slow Night in Ginza

Pelicans of Japantown

The Rain in Nagoya

Smoke in a Blameless Language

The Summer We Watched all the Godzillas

A Spy in the House of Manju

Shimoyama and the Absent Ghost

A Good Place to Leave a Lover

FROM THE MOMENT she arrived at the park, the insects made everything worse. The mosquitoes were on the prowl and the air hummed with the cicadas that were calling away, unthinking, a lascivious drone in the trees. She had come early and strolled around for as long as the heat allowed, then sat down on a bench in the shade and slipped off her sweaty sandals. Her nerves weren't impressed, but at least she had tried.

It was August, the holidays coming up.

The sky was awfully blue.

She could oversee the whole concourse, an oval of dirt and cement, one eye on the new arrivals that came from the nearby station. Her apartment was walking distance, and while the heat had put the kibosh on her habit of morning runs, she still loved the small neighborhood park. The site used to house an army sanatorium, a dark complex that had been shuttered due to certain unfortunate rumors, things that were done to Koreans. Some said the park was still haunted, spooked by ghosts of the former patients who had languished in the sanatorium. Even strolling on moonless nights, though, she hadn't found more cause for alarm than an owl perching on a tree, watching her moves. She loved how the park was a world of its own, the shade of the canopied paths and the bamboo at rest in the grove, no breeze stirring the evening calm. A good place, she assumed, to leave a lover and not look back.

The first company men left the station, a suburb in the Tokyo northeast that came alive when the offices let out. The men dressed in identical fashion, dark pants and white shirt, a cooling shirt underneath, a look that always reminded her of the private religious schools back East. They seemed slow as they headed home, too slow even in the heat. As if there were things on their mind, a problem they had to address. No matter the various efforts, the exports and policy tweaks, the yen remained weak to the dollar. Or was it something else, something that no one could guess?

The kids weren't fazed by the temperature, since this was the summer they knew. Two boys played a game of tennis, their bicycles used for a net in a corner of the concrete concourse. No supervision, both parents at work, the boys roamed without hats in the sun that hammered down on the concrete. A vending machine behind them, sturdy and blue, offered drinks with hammered-down prices. Bong badumbong—voilà, your iced coffee.

She was done and the fault wasn't hers; she hadn't done anything wrong. She didn't care about zodiac matches, the traits of her sign and the stuff they said in her horoscope, the way she supposedly acted in love.

Anyway, she was a Scorpio.

Loyal and unforgiving.

Having weighed the thing until dawn in between sips of wine and a long walk to an all-night store, she had resolved at last she would leave. Her heart had moved on, as the Japanese say. She wasn't the person he imagined, and with absolute drunken clarity that had shocked her with implications, she knew it could not be a long-term thing. No way she could be with a man who would turn her into an object, a woman he thought he could mold based on his personal taste. She was stupid for getting involved and embarrassed on her own time, never mind there was some sort of chemistry, how they might match in some other ways. Which, of course, was how the thing had started.

Her work at the company was so dull, her tasks so absurdly repetitive that even a machine might have asked politely if there wasn't something else it could do. They didn't need an American, not for hours of data entry, and yet, here she was stuck in Japan at a company that hadn't changed much since the days of the Eisenhower administration, punching mindlessly in and out and keeping her name tag visible, in fact, visible *at all times*, as the manager had admonished. How they loved to watch and admonish, to check every single detail, then check one more time, and then—yes!—admonish. She thought that it was the mindlessness, the reserve of the office and the attitude of her peers who were acting all buttoned-down and then shot her those smoldering looks, that were making her think about sex. Like, a lot. Her soul almost numb from the dullness, the rules that somehow made her horny and ache for some kind of transgression, she would stare into empty space when, in strange primal leaps, her mind was assailed by fantasies that were shockingly raw and explicit. A few seconds would see her slip from the data in spreadsheet columns to outrageousness in a love hotel. Anything to make her feel good, less hopeless down in her soul.

The moment they met in a hallway—a client who glanced at her curiously as he stepped out of a corner suite—she knew she had found her escape. A Japanese man, a tall drink of water. The scar on his cheek absorbed her with hints of a secret past.

A kendo swordsman? A swashbuckler? Had he brawled in Shinjuku alleys over gambling debts or a girl?

"Not sure if he likes me. It feels so ambiguous."

"He likes you plenty," her coworker laughed. "That's why

it's ambiguous."

"What if he . . ."

"You should move quick. He is popular, I can tell."

His confidence made her hesitate, the mix of money and looks. A man who moved with the grace of a cat, Toru knew he was handsome in a way that was almost classical. High cheekbones and deep brown eyes, a mustache shading his upper lip. His clothes were new and clean-cut in the fashion of conservative finance, although he loathed his conservative father, a financier with a nasty temper who treated women as personal maids. Toru worked hard and enjoyed his success and its fruits, the penthouse loft in Roppongi and the lifestyle of a corporate consultant, with a sort of gleeful materialism in a system designed for him. He agreed that graduating from Keio, a private university in Tokyo that funneled students along from kindergarten without having to take any tests, made him part of a privileged elite.

"If you can get it," he laughed, "why feel sheepish?" The entitlement irked her, the importance he placed on money as the sole means to get respect.

Agreeing for once with his father, Toru thought it was time for Japan to amend the old post-war constitution, to strengthen the security forces to the ways of a normal military. He said that soldiers who had to wait until they were able to return the fire, reliant on help from America the moment when things became tough, were a joke that no one respected. He said Americans would not understand, and she said, "I want to. Can you help me understand?" But for some reason, he never helped.

These were the things she knew about him. Besides what he liked to eat and the way he liked to be touched.

A boy on the concourse was practicing pitches, throwing balls only he could see at a batter who wasn't there. His shorts barely covered his thighs, scrawny and pale in the heat. Unaware he was being watched as he stepped on the plate again, the boy weighed the ball in his hand, readying for the pitch. He had eyed the boys playing tennis, perhaps wondering if he could join in a non-racket-owning capacity. The players, however, ignored him completely. They didn't want him in their tennis game and didn't need any referee, and a boy from another school might as well be green with antennae.

The boy in shorts threw the phantom ball, his hand letting go and sending it flying. A line that was perfect, a pitch destined for a no-hitter and roaring cheers in the bleachers, an offer from the Seibu Lions. The boy knew about ten thousand hours and requirements for the major league, solemn-faced and no time for girls.

Their first lunch was at Tokyo Dome, her first date that wasn't American. Toru was late, which irked her, but she soon found herself charmed by his style, an easy unassuming presence so unlike his business panache. The way he sat there, almost still and with eyes that listened, rarely mentioning himself or his work. The way he sipped on the wine, then studied the label thoughtfully. The warm eyes, the wet wipes he used on his face, mopping sweat off his perfect skin that she imagined tasted like salt. They were advertising, she realized, the American seated outside with a tall, handsome Japanese. It didn't bother her; she liked the attention as she forked her penne puttanesca, eating quite a bit faster than him and somehow still talking more. Only Toru seemed mildly embarrassed to see passersby stopping and staring, then entering into the restaurant to see what the place was about.

"They always do this," he sighed. "As if Americans make a place cool."

He hated the worship, the mindless embrace of the people who had dropped unforgivable bombs, then made millions of dollars with movies that pondered the moral weight. He didn't know what would hit him later in a room at a pink hotel, a place with all sorts of mirrors that rented per night and per hour. She blamed the wine, the summer air warm on her skin, the allure of the smooth physique that hummed behind his designer shirt, when ambiguity ceased in the room and she had stayed on top till exhaustion, a cicada in helpless heat. She herself was surprised, almost shocked. She wasn't like that, not back home, not even in her college days. He took her shopping the following day, an afternoon they both enjoyed, then they returned to the pink hotel—the same room, buttons pressed to receive the key, then cash for the invisible receptionist—where Toru watched the new dress come off in the sheen of a bulbous lamp. His face held a sense of rapture, a man seeing snow for the first time in his life. She hadn't known she could make these sounds until a neighbor had knocked on the wall, seriously, can you keep it down, guys?

He was late, perhaps held up with a client. No message, no response to her texts, and already, it was six fifteen. Her nerves were starting to hum as the park was suffused with ambiguity. How many couples were saying goodbye today in Tokyo and the rest of the world? And why the hell was he late?

She didn't know how the Japanese handled breakups, but she feared she might lose control of the script that she had prepared. So strange how a few short words could remove someone from your life and turn them into a ghost, a memory to fade away. She stumbled in her resolve. Without the affair and its comfort, there was no more reason to be here, no more point in staying in Tokyo and living the same as before. And with no point in remaining here and no point in returning home, what was the point in being anywhere at all if she wasn't able to make things last? She had longed for some sort of meaning, had wanted to learn how to stay and find peace in a lasting commitment, because she knew if she couldn't learn this, she would keep losing people forever. However, Japan hadn't solved any problems. The wrong man and the church bells silent, the years she would never get back while Japanese people kept guessing her age.

The job held no more escape, and the numbers, oh no, the numbers, they were stealing a piece of her soul every time she punched in again. No matter what happened with Toru from here, she didn't want to end up alone to make shopping fill up empty weekends, the emptiness in her heart. She had seen the Shibuya women, the bags and the shuffle, the unfocused eyes in the streets. The thought made her shiver.

A man talked on his phone in passing, disbelief in his voice. An attempted murder, a politician gunned down near Kyoto and rushed to the emergency room. She whipped out her phone and scrolled as the story was breaking in international news, a shocking event in Japan. The gunman had been arrested; the country was holding its breath. No one knew what to say in response to an official shot in the streets, a political assassination that now was a part of the park.

The boy in shorts paused his practice, after a fastball that made batters weep. Oblivious to his surroundings and the evening chime in the park, the announcement on the old speakers telling the time to go home, he now glanced at the clock on the concourse and remembered that home meant dinner. Leaving the ball where it landed invisibly, he clambered on his rusty bicycle, then pedaled away down the path.

It was then, looking after the boy rushing home, that she was struck by the realization that Toru would never come. She wouldn't see him again—not today, and not ever. She was shocked, then almost relieved, as the thing began to make sense.

It wasn't that he lost his nerve or was carelessly standing her up; it wasn't like him to be rude. What if, ever the guarded strategist, he had quietly beaten her to it, avoiding the scene he saw coming from the way they had parted last night? His request had upset her—a thing she had never done, wasn't sure that she even liked, or was ready to try. Too soon, he was moving too fast. More upsetting perhaps was the fact that she had taken some time to consider, that, in a moment of stupid embarrassment, she had thought about trying the thing before misgivings had made her refuse. Was he seeing her as a trophy, taking her already for granted? Was he bragging to his business buddies about how American women were easy, how they did everything you asked? As their argument grew involved and meandered to national pride, a thing she never thought might feature in a row she had with a lover, they reached a deeper, more resonant level of bitterness that made her voice turn suddenly sharp, a shriek of offended defense, until alarm bells rang in her mind to warn that a line had been crossed. "Are we going there?" she wondered anxiously, and once you wonder, you are always there.

Toru hated scenes, she had seen it, any conflict or confrontation that might make him feel the least bit awkward. He seldom shared his feelings or thoughts, while her bluntness could make him flinch. She had liked his reticent pride, which she thought was part of his class. His absence might mean his consent, a clean break to end what they had. No drama and tears and fumbling through speeches, not even as much as a text. Much easier to be firm and delicate without any interaction, without facing the other side and what they might think or need. A swipe without sound, then loose ends forever.

She looked around one last time, then picked up her bag and rose. Seven o'clock, the air had started to cool. The shade of the trees moved in on the boys who had readied to leave.

The area was residential, narrow streets with old curtained shops and houses, an art college near the station. Off the park was a school with a yard, the students gone for the day. From a window on the second floor came the sound of a gentle piano, resounding in the empty building in a way that now touched her heart. A theme by Chopin, amateurishly earnest. She imagined a girl with small hands, one of thousands of middle school girls who sat down for practice between homework and dinner, sitting perfectly straight on her chair and sighing at each mistake. She saw the notes floating out of a window like bubbles in a dream by Chopin, then smashing against a tree or landing in the dusty yard. This was real, she mused, a part of the history of the world.

Reluctantly, she made for the exit, to get home in time for the tears. The park was so calm, she could have sat here all night and gazed at the faraway stars, the cicadas under the moon, the bamboo swaying their leaves in the breeze like gossipy ladies at tea. Perhaps sometime in the small hours, the time when the night was strangest, a twig might snap in the dark and then Toru would appear before her, a ghost from the old sanatorium asking her on a walk.

Her skin was damp as she checked her phone. No message or updates on the politician, no motive for the murder attempt coming seemingly out of the blue. The country was paused, numbed in the heat, and none of the experts had explanations or knew where to go from here. The mood gauge of an ancient nation had leaped from somnolent calm to disorder, an eruption of violence and blood on the sunny sidewalks of peace. She didn't care about politics here, not even the man who was dead, and yet she was touched by a sense of loss, a sudden disorientation, as if the ground under her feet had shifted into a soft, unreliable mess. Her mind went to Toru, her thoughts making her sweat. Why had she left him after one fight, adding more emptiness to her life? Why had she protected her time and heart when they weren't needed for anything else?

She couldn't text him or even call—that wasn't how ghosting worked and, anyway, she was probably blocked. She now desperately wanted to see him, to talk to him on this day leaving his country in a strange new place. He admired the politician, had mentioned him several times, because he looked good playing golf on a course and commanded respect when he spoke. Because he was tough and old-fashioned and had called for a stronger defense, a Japan standing up for itself in a world of perilous unknowns.

The dresses were always lovely, although never exactly her choice. They were feminine in a way she had shunned, a way she hadn't known was safe or might suit her own personal style. Her peers saw the change right away—a blossoming, one called it with a wink—as she showed up to work in short skirts or a playful pastel design, slim halter necklines and stylish culottes. Somehow in

Japan, it all worked, never felt like she was trying too hard as the fabrics enveloped her figure, expenses be damned. She followed Toru to Ginza and then later to Aoyama avenues, the boutiques on Omotesando that catered to more mature tastes. He had a keen eye and knew where to go—the staff familiar from prior visits and shoppers with deeper pockets, she never asked when or with whom—and would pick up the tabs discreetly as she kept checking herself in a mirror.

She hadn't done this before, never tried clothes on with a man watching; in fact, she had never been fashionable. A thing of delight, it turned out, the most fun in her life in a while. Toru wasn't creepy or weird, never insisted on having his way. He just knew what he liked when he saw it. He might suggest a match or a color with genuine interest in the result, then give his opinion on how she looked. She loved stepping out of the fitting room and turning for him in a dress, the way he would smile with approval. She loved when his eyes lit up because of a costume or wraparound silk, the attention and constant assurance that a Japanese man found her beautiful. Other shoppers were stealing glances that made her feel like another person, a woman enchanting a man without any use of words.

"A bit daring, a bit unusual," a clerk once said as she left, two shopping bags at her side. "But an American pulls it off."

A Human Accident

THE AIR STALLED in the rainy season, ceased to move altogether. Not even the showers coming for weeks could relieve the tropical choke, a lassitude numbing the days, then keeping you up at night.

"What is the degree of her hesitation?" At the Todai café, Shingo sipped his iced coffee. "On a scale from one to six, where is she?"

I put down the *International Herald Tribune*. The pages were damp in the heat, weeping for American sins.

"Maybe a four. Three point five."

"It's like a woman. On the fence about everything." Shingo sighed, then his face grew serious. "How do you know that she likes you?"

"The messages, late at night. She keeps asking all kinds of questions."

"How late at night?"

"Sometimes midnight. Or even later."

Shingo looked impressed. "That is different. Until midnight, the world is watching. A message after that is serious."

"I should be careful. There's been a bad experience already."

"Please do not cause any suffering. Not in this awful heat."

Among the members in my American Culture class at Hitachi, Shingo was the most outspoken. The other ones were like typewriters—you had to pound on them to elicit words. We sat in Shinjuku at lunchtime, watching office ladies and salarymen issue innumerably from machines of work, a stream of pedestrians watching their spaces and steps, maneuvering, shifting, never changing the flow of the mass. Noodle-shop regulars slurped up lunch-hour minutes, while magazine men and dolls with expensive eyes, the disciples of Seibu and Mitsukoshi, were out shopping for goods that gave meaning. It was Tokyo, the mother of buzz. In spite of the movement that never eased, everything appeared calm in a gentle and comforting way, as though each of the million beings were supported by a network of loyal peers, as though none of the people and structures could ever be any different. A Legoland full of humans, fueled by a dreamless industry.

It was the calm I had craved. San Francisco is kicking and screaming when America invades other countries, and everything had become too much. I had fled the turmoil at home, the hawks that pushed for more strikes and kept shouting down everyone else, the rallies I attended for months in ever-diminishing hope, until the day when boots hit the ground and the missiles soared through the air. I collapsed in a bathroom that day, surrendered and sick to my soul. A man who couldn't change anything, a fool learning the ways of the world.

Love it or leave it, so I left when Hitachi was hiring. The economy still in a slump, there were billboards all over town showing temples in beautiful landscapes and cherry trees in full bloom, promising a good life if you tried something new. *Pink slips over here? Pink salmon over there!*

My late twenties and I set sail, away from the spams of empire. I never told anyone or admitted it to myself, but I had hopes for the great abroad. To lose myself in the strangeness, then come out improved, reborn.

One table over sat a little princess, a puffball of pink that was smitten with French rococo, her hair a short yearning blonde. She stared at a piece of raspberry cheesecake that sat like a brick on her plate, untouched since she had taken a picture. She might have ordered the cake as support, a defense against some sort of darkness, because she suddenly started to sigh, and her eyes slipped away into gloom. A shadow fell on her cheeks, her lips pressed together tightly.

Shingo nodded, having noticed the woman as well. Smoothing his tie to get back to work, he cleared his throat matter-of-factly.

"We Japanese are very careful with each other. We have to be."

The most careful of them all was Megumi. On our strolls to the Emperor's Palace, she would quietly watch the turtles, the way they swam through the moat and then sunned on the rocks for hours. A timeless creature herself, every move that she made seemed measured, as if objects like tables and chairs, even the spaces her small frame traversed, could be easily dented or bruised. In the morning, afraid that a run to the station would leave her soaked in the heat, she allowed two hours' time to wake up and get dressed. In between smokes and two cups of coffee, weather forecasts and pop music on the radio, she brushed her hair like a chore of vision. Each stroke would receive attention as it moved through her pageboy cut, each stocking becoming a project as it covered a short, white leg. Once, when I asked her, "What are you thinking?" Megumi looked up, surprised, as if the question were foreign to her. "Just now? I don't know . . . nothing special."

Her eyes were silent, letting things be what they were. One day, I had lunch with a colleague—nothing serious, but she was cute and curious about Americans—and so as not to alarm Megumi, I made an excuse about meeting my boss. A half-assed lie, but I thought it would keep things simple. I learned the hard way not to lie to a Japanese woman, and never again.

American women, always ready to smell a rat, always eager

to check the facts and explode into angry scenes, assail you with endless questions to get at the truth and the bottom of things, letting you see where the lie needs support. In other words, they cooperate. Megumi, on the other hand, seemed unmoved by the spell of language, the stooge of the two-timing male. She wasn't chasing after the truth or aiming to get to the bottom, didn't think it could ever be reached. Her eyes on mine as she listened, she unnerved me with sheer ambiguity, as if her silence meant she was on. I made the mistake of the amateur cheat: never embellish the humbug with details. Yapping away without a response, I lost faith in the power of words to make anyone believe in anything, when at last, pleading for a crumb of trust, I slipped on a contradiction and sailed down a deep hole of mess. When at last I came up for air, Megumi lowered her eyes and said softly, with a note of disappointment still haunting my dreams, "I will believe you." That was all. I canceled the coworker lunch—more feeble excuses, no questions—and vowed never again to meet with another woman.

Her plainness calmed me, made me simple as well. I didn't have to be special or brilliant, didn't need to impress her friends or see greatness ahead in my future. Megumi just wanted presence, as much as there was, grounded in everydayness. I once asked her why she was with me, why she would ruffle her Zen composure with a man so upset about preemptive strikes and the ignorance of the masses, so deeply at odds with the way the world was. I searched for a guide, a clue as to how to be with her, fishing for compliments in a sea of hush. But when her answer came promptly, without any thought, it was oddly without satisfaction. "Because you are kind."

If love was that simple, then why was she holding back?

She was holding back because I was too, because of the air-conditioned apartment and the things that were stuffed in her fridge. The time she had spent in the coop was never that much of an issue.

The casino was in Shibuya, so accessible to the public that not even etiquette called it secret. Megumi had flunked out of college and was dealing at a blackjack table in a uniform necktie and vest, as if that were where she belonged. She was a good dealer, she said, never cheated, never lost control of a table, and she loved working in what the Japanese call the night world. The stakes and the drinks and the atmosphere of the place, the regulars who tipped her handsomely and the comradery among a staff of misfits, the cash envelopes in the morning which she would spend within days on new clothes and restaurants—all this gave her a sense of excitement. The best part, she said, was the walk after work to the station, the empty Shibuya crossing at dawn.

The raid was unsporting, a shock to the canned interactions between Japanese police and the yakuza. As a rule, Megumi explained, crackdowns were leaked in a timely manner to all the parties affected, easing the awkwardness inherent in a police raid. Did the cops leave their shoes at the door, I mused, aligning them in a row before charging in through the entrance?

All neat and tidy? All right—going in!

That night was different, a nasty surprise. Megumi was caught in a string of arrests and spent three months in a jail for women, where it dawned on her what it means to be charged with an actual crime. An hour southwest of Tokyo, it was a complex for low-security. A cell without windows or furniture, but not bad for a jail in Japan. Adhering to yakuza rule, Megumi stayed mum during interrogations that had everyone going through motions. Small fish, the casino bosses assured, were tossed back into the sea. Her mother came to visit one day, a stash of manga and mumbled news in a long, awkward hour of looking through bars and hearing about her new cat, a rascal who was full of mischief.

"No word about this," her mom said in leaving, "to anyone else in the family." Megumi may not have been forgiven—perhaps because, in Japan, only losers got caught in a raid. The prosecutor dropped all charges and tossed her back into the sea, her new life as a woman marked. Ashamed to the bone, desperate to be good.

For most people, this isn't the stuff of first dates. But Megumi was different. She confessed it all over drinks—"There is something I need to tell you"—as if it were some sort of dating requirement she had to get out of the way. I didn't care about her Tokyo past and there was no way that I would have found out; but then, convinced that I needed to know, she didn't stop talking until it was all off her chest. *This is me, the most shameful thing that ever happened. Still wish to proceed, my new friend?*

The worst were the exercise and bathing hours, she remembered, when you weren't allowed to speak or even look at the other inmates. Although never much of a talker, Megumi was scared by the isolation, the eerily silent halls and workrooms that weren't meant to correct, just punish and shame. Moving only as they were told, inmates stood numbly beside each other with no chance to reach out or even acknowledge another presence. "We were like ghosts," Megumi said, her eyes dark. "Locked in a ghost house for women."

The bellicose nature of current events had rendered my culture class awkward. As I lectured from the *Stateside* textbook—where Steve and Rose Miller tipped the waitress kindly, watched the Super Bowl together with Grandpa, and lived, as a rule, like hardworking decent people according to scripture and democracy—the war was the elephant in the room. No one called me out as a hypocrite, but as the members took notes and nodded without seeming to agree, as the occasional frown betrayed their unease about moves of the land of the free, about deaths justifiable to the Millers, I sensed more and more that I failed to connect and keep it simple and human. Doubling down with more helpless blabber, I finished the class soaked in sweat. Another American hard at work, going about it exactly the wrong way.

Hitachi arranged for my housing, a room in a guesthouse the size of a spacious shoebox. A sink and a single stove plate, etched from decades of soy sauce. A futon on the matted floor, a squat toilet in the hallway; the ceiling so awfully low I had acquired a guarded stoop. The whole house knew when the foreigner arrived, my head meeting the wooden frame like chimes cussing at eight o'clock.

Upstairs lived an office lady, who liked to wear orange dresses. In the morning as she left for work, the hem of her skirt would swish down the hall, then heels clacked along the stairs. Hearing her shut the door to her room, I would jump out of bed and sit by the window, my eyes following her in the sun as she emerged on the street, then rushed gracefully to the subway. A beautiful rose, late for work.

Most foreigners were struck by the women you saw in endless parades à la mode, the impeccable Tokyo fashions that were squished on the morning trains. The whole town had a feminine feel, despite the punishing workloads that had people toil until midnight. The women were playful and enjoyed the attention, without showing any active desire. In a way, they were cats; they liked to be near you and purr and see what might happen next. I looked at them with different eyes than I had for the women back home. As if you could love them safely, as if their feminine warmth could make you accept that, really, they wanted a family. Now one of them was right here, upstairs in my building: *Go up, say hello and be kind; be a lucky American dog.* Sinking back with a sigh on the futon, I imagined the rose without orange.

The house manager was Korean, a young, bearded hipster who strummed his guitar and drank shochu to pass the nights. The whole place could have burned to the ground and the manager might have kept strumming, peacefully smashed and enjoying the stars in a loving, cosmic embrace. Having met the worst sort of foreigners, he believed he could see right through me.

"You came for the culture?" he asked with a smirk, thinking of Western men chasing girls in discos of silent heartbreak, the spoils of Roppongi nights. Then he saw the novels stacked on the floor, the thumbed classics by Mishima and Tanizaki right at home on the musty tatami, my Japanese dictionaries and the album on Kurosawa movies. He raised an arched eyebrow, surprised.

"Of course," I said, no longer sure. "I'm all about culture."

I hadn't known what I should expect, but then life in Japan was easy. A warm, pleasant bubble bath, the bubbles eager to please. The absence of noise was a boon, the way you were left alone and could sit in a park and read. No one mentioned current events, like it wasn't even a thing; no sarcastic or clever remarks or opinions that were strongly held, besides how to make the best ramen. Instead, there were bows from clerks in the stores, apologies for the poor English. The food was healthier than back home, though in the first few months I had frowned over bowel movements that were suddenly shaped like seahorses. Octopus snacks and seaweed could do that to a man from Antelope, a small town in California that no Japanese ever knew.

Nights had me lying awake in the heat, thinking difficult thoughts about the showtime in the Middle East. An invasion, a domination, the machine-governed hell that my taxes unleashed with its missiles and tanks and bombs. I was afraid to turn on the television: there were lies and dead people in there, sidewalks screaming and disemboweled while palm trees swayed in a breeze, then cut to a show with Japanese people slipping food into happy mouths, eyes closed and orgasm faces.

I couldn't accept the America I was part of, or the fact that, however conflicted, I had to share my country with others. A mass of unruly individuals, desiring and pushing and scheming and in numberless needy ways contouring America's meaning, the sum of its deeds and effects and its consequences for the world, some so horribly wrong that I marched in the streets holding signs and got arrested for failure to disperse. A fool, a person apart—absurd and incomprehensible.

I didn't know what to do with America; all I knew was I couldn't return, not now, to the scene of the crime. Remote in my chosen exile, away from the tainted home and the orphaned limbs of Iraqi Freedom, I thanked Hitachi for the ticket to Legoland.

Between lotus root and sashimi, Megumi and I fell in love. Wordlessly, unavoidably, a vignette for the waiter to witness. The place was Shibuya, a candle-lit sphere revolving up in the sky, overlooking the urban expanse. Steel and glass as far as the eye could reach, flecked with lights that would shine on reports all night. Overtime loyalties, the heroes of work—*wait, am I grinding my teeth?* In the distance was Tokyo Tower, red and white and a little pointless, something silly we need in our souls. Down a canyon of office spaces, a fenced patch of lawn held a dreamy escape. Floodlit specks playing golf amid thousands of busy lives.

"You've been here before?" I asked when we ordered the food.

"Back in my twenties, a party at the casino. I ended up here with another dealer."

"A date?"

"A young girl from Chiba." Megumi smiled at the question. "We sat here all night, enjoying the view and talking. Her dream was to see the skyline and send pictures to all her friends. It is countryside dream."

I tried for her eyes across the low table and was drawn into hazel warmth. But mixed with the warmth was reserve, as if a cute thing had seen the world, met some characters and trusted them, and learned that cute things had to watch their backside. Especially in a jailhouse for women.

Most of her story was filling in gaps. A child of the 1980s, the bubble economy in Japan when fortunes were amassed and lost in a manner of happy delirium. Her parents ran a Japanese restaurant, where you could order the coffee with gold dust and the champagne cost a current month's salary. It was Babylon, sushi-style. When the party crashed in the '90s, Megumi became a part of what the Japanese call *ushinawareta junen*—a decade lost to recession that spawned a new lost generation. Not as picturesque, mind you, as the war-hardened types roaming Paris in the 1920s, sipping red wine in artsy cafés and discussing the need for new realism. But as Japanese youth looked around in the post-bubble slump, they shared the same disillusion, the sense that the old ways no longer worked. No more shopping sprees in the Ginza, closets stuffed with designer bags. No more sacrifice for the companies that were ruthlessly grinding you down and gave you a watch for retirement. The '90s saw the rise of the temp and those opting out of the race, the young abandoning outdated lifestyles of quiet suburban despair. Uninvested in the rewards, unwilling to sell their souls to the needs of the corporate engine.

With a criminal record and no skills besides dealing cards, Megumi was glad to find work as a temp, a non-regular employee feeding data into a computer. She didn't see how these jobs killed careers, half the salary and without any benefits, without hopes of ever advancing no matter how often she made tea for the boss. Just like that, in one move, she was stuck.

Now at thirty-two and still single, in a country obsessed with motherhood and seeing all of the daughters married, she was an object of much concern and marked with the thoughtless malice of convention as a leftover Christmas cake, an item beyond twenty-four and therefore of lesser value. A Christmas cake after Christmas, however discounted, appeals mostly to those indifferent to the preferences of the mainstream. Enter Western Man to the rescue, a lover of cake universally, to pick up the cakes that the Japanese spurned. Yum, Christmas cake.

The boyfriend of seven years had bailed out before commitment, a move that men make that everyone hates. No parents had cushioned her fall, no close friends or hobbies or things that gave meaning to life. She had favorites, however, a day out at Disney Sea and rides at the mermaid lagoon, or renting a car and then driving all night, her favorite songs on the speakers as Tokyo zoomed past. More than anything, she liked weekends in bed watching movies from a shop right next to her building. No Kurosawa, but comedies from America, the sillier the better.

"When you are watching TV by yourself, do you laugh when there is something funny?" she asked when the food arrived.

She looked out the window that reached to the ceiling, her eyes reflecting the neon outside. One booth over, a couple flirted elliptically over sushi.

"Some comedians, perhaps some slapstick." I fumbled with the eel on my plate. "I might think that something is funny, but not really laugh."

Megumi nodded. "I was worried it might be strange. I don't wanna act strange when I'm alone. That is why I check."

"You watch a lot of TV?"

Again, the code of omission. Her eyes slipped into mine and probed, assessing reception, then decided to send a message full of deep emotion and thought, a telepathic appeal too private, too obscurely complex, to be entrusted to grammar and words. "If only you knew," they appeared to say, and my eyes called back, "Hey, what happened?" A man of language, alas, I had no means to decode her signal, no clue what she tried to express.

"Maybe . . ." she said, her eyes leaving mine at last. And that was the end of that.

We stalled the goodbye at the subway until our lips met in impartial neon. Her face close to mine and the smell of shampoo in the air, Megumi whispered, "I had a nice time. Thanks for the evening and dinner."

She smiled uncertainly before starting down the long steps, her Hermès bag swinging at her side. Before rounding an underground corner, she stopped and turned for a final wave, the way Japanese people do, then turned again and made for the Ginza line.

I stumbled along on the sidewalk, embraced by the warmth of the herd. Afloat on the crush that moved as a unit, a murmurous stream oozing home or along to more karaoke, I stopped at the curb with everyone else, then moved when the others did. A new mass poured out from an exit, an impassable human wall. No way to cross, so I let myself drift, no destination in mind. The hum of the herd couldn't shape any words, but there was a sense of communal cheer, a charm that went beyond language. Men in shirtsleeves and ties, some rushing with phones to their ears and nodding their understanding, while women were sharing a laugh as their work for the day was done, comparing vacations and food or lamenting the summer heat.

There was comfort in sameness, in being like everyone else. Towering over the crowd like an emblem of the exceptionalism of the most careless people on earth, I wished I could fold myself into the whole. I longed to be smaller and less conspicuous, less clumsily consequential in the mass of my six-foot frame. I never meant to be large like this, afraid any move might break something small and send people running away, afraid I would be on the news that had everyone roll their eyes and ask, "What the hell did he break this time?" More than anything, floating down endless avenues in the warmth of the summer night, I wished to hold on to the deep sense of peace. To that end, I needed Megumi, had to be there when she watched her movies.

We spent the next weeks just going on dates and slowly getting to know each other, until one night it had gotten so late that Megumi stayed over at the guesthouse, much to the delight of the Korean manager, who now gave me smiles and thumbs up in the hallway as a welcome into some sort of club. Not so different from dating in America, I thought, until the day I stayed at her place and things became a lot more serious.

"*Irasshaimase*," chimed the welcome in the store, a reflex from the two clerks, both youngsters in smelly uniforms who were stocking the shelves with sandwiches. For some reason, this time it bugged me.

"I want to shake them sometimes and yell, 'You are robots! All of you!'"

Megumi had joined the students who were crowding the magazine stand, reading manga they would never purchase.

"Perhaps they will answer," her voice turned cheerfully mechanic, "'We are enjoying being robots. It is safe.'"

She smiled at her own words, surprised she had said something funny. I went over and kissed her smile without any explanation. A synopsis of modern Japan.

The whole day had been perfect. We had cycled in Ueno Park, where we fed *senbei* to carps in the pond and then moved on from shade to shade counting couples who walked their dogs. Megumi said there were four, but one was a Chihuahua, which I quipped was an accessory, not a dog, and then Megumi asked the meaning of *accessory*, and I said, "Never mind, four." Now we were headed for her apartment, my first visit there, two weeks after dinner in the sky over Shibuya.

A quiet street lined with cherry trees, serene in the afternoon. A ramen shop with a curtained entrance, next to a store for musical instruments that also repaired shamisen. There were old, wooden houses, some likely from before the war, plus an apartment complex from the '70s, which, in Tokyo, was equally old. I saw futons on narrow balconies that tenants had put out to air and absorb the smell of the sun, and as we came to a DVD shop and the bins with tapes on the sidewalk, I knew this must be the place.

The building was next to a neighborhood graveyard, overlooking the rows of the graves. The smell of warm wood and incense came up to the small apartment, adding solemnness to the heat. An old woman in a plain dress was cleaning an obelisk headstone, drawing water from a nearby basin and scrubbing the stone with a rag. She wanted the grave to be clean when her ancestors came to visit. Beside some of the graves was a stand with tall wooden slats, clattering softly in the evening breeze. The inscriptions carved on the slats, Megumi explained, bore the Buddhist name of the dead.

She hadn't told me she roomed with Doraemon, a robot cat from the twenty-second century. The thing adorned mugs and sheets and the sliding door to the bedroom, the sole homey touch in a place that was otherwise bare, empty as broken dreams.

"When people know that you like an anime..."—Megumi slipped out of her sandals— "they all give you things with that character."

"What does he do? Save the earth from injustice and war?"

"His friend is Nobita, a boy who is always in trouble. Doraemon helps with his magic pocket."

"A blue cat with a propeller. No ears."

"Robot mice ate his ears." Megumi was serious. "Doraemon was shocked and turned blue, then never changed back. It is anime story."

The fridge in the kitchen held further surrealism. The top shelf had toy figurines of faded plastic stacked up on magazines, next to flacons of nail polish and makeup, while the middle shelf was empty save for some napkins. In the bins at the bottom, a scuffed old cell phone and charger were squished beside panties and balled-up socks.

"What the...?" I stared at inedibles.

Megumi looked at the fridge, her small forehead hardened. The machine hummed away in the silence, cooling the socks and toys.

"It was getting waste, always empty. I put things in to save electricity."

"How about eggs or some mayonnaise? Of course, vegetables are ambitious."

"I never cook, and then it goes bad. The convenience store is my fridge now."

She didn't say it was better than prison food, but it was somewhere there in her voice. Her eyes became glazed, withdrew to a place where a dark rain falls on empty apartments. Inside there are shells of our clueless endeavors, an oblivion to which we lose people we desperately need, spooked forever by ghosts who once knew us.

I asked him to leave because I loved him so much, much more than he loved me. I thought better to be lonely than marry the wrong man. After that, I was crazy for a while; it hurt and it was so terrible. But the terrible became smaller, and now I started to forget.

Megumi checked a bump on my forehead, a new endowment from the wooden doorframe, which somehow segued to love on the futon. She was shy as a rule, held back in her slender frame and particular about how to be touched, but this time she was urging against me, a clumsy seal full of love. The words of surrender she whispered, her hands on my silent face, sealed a pact made before with eyes only. Nearing climax, however, she stopped, as if to be spared what was next. Something about her reluctance, the fear that had seized her body, made me wonder if she had ever experienced it with someone beside her. She slipped away and curved in, as if trying to disappear, her fingers opening and closing on the robot cat on the sheets. Not a breeze stirred as she trembled, feeling for something, a hold in the world.

The night came in from the balcony—the graves down below, the metropolis humming beyond. From next door came a pop song, then a heavy thud on the floor. What was happening in the houses of Tokyo? I ached to reach out to Megumi and touch the shimmering skin that was far away, but I feared she might crack into pieces. Breathing next to her and listening in the dark to what sounded like muffled sobs, I sensed her gazing at the TV, the remote control and the air conditioner on the wall, the things she used daily in her solitary rituals and was summoning now for help.

Pity came to my stomach like illness. I saw that Megumi needed me to stay but that pride wouldn't let her ask, that she needed saving from the apartment where deep prison quiet was eased by a surface of cuteness. A place where emptiness had a lived-in quality, where she wouldn't cook and watched too much TV and then coped with that life by eating convenience store meals and stuffing the fridge with old toys; the place her ex-boyfriend—over-loved and over-needed—had been asked to abandon when Megumi couldn't stand her own feelings.

Therefore, my hesitation. It didn't seem fair, the way we were suddenly fated and the stakes had been raised toward marriage, urged by a woman made selfish by the way her society worked.

A little breaking was required here. Perhaps more than that.

"Japan has no secrets, not really," Shingo explained at the Today café. "Everybody knows everything, the rest is pretending we don't."

He rattled the ice in his coffee as if this could create a breeze. It was lunch break and the heat meant business, hitting us with new resolve as we toasted the end of the course.

"It's clear you feel pressured. She doesn't like it. She wants a partner, not a man who feels sorry."

"Whatever she wants, she doesn't say. How am I supposed to know what things mean?"

Shingo laughed wryly, then sighed. "My wife makes my lunchbox, five days a week. She lays out my clothes in the morning, sometimes on weekends. I am sure she will fight to the death to protect our marriage and children. Only sometimes, I wonder if she likes me. It cannot be helped, I suppose. I mean, I suppose that is marriage."

I mopped sweat off my face, too absorbed in myself to be shocked to hear Shingo was married. I couldn't stop thinking of Megumi. Was the relationship a mistake from the start? Had I walked into something bigger, a system of social rules that I couldn't hope to understand in this life, only to break her heart yet again?

Outside, the masses were flowing routinely. People crowded the shade of the awnings, shunning the glare that punished the streets. A television set on the wall had news from the showtime. The war had been fought and decisively won, yet all I could hear from the commentary were the name of a town in ashes and the words "overwhelming use of force." Then up on the screen, a face that I knew.

He looked strange in the air-force flight suit. A middle-aged man with gray hair, climbing out of a fighter jet and stepping onto an aircraft carrier. His helmet propped at the waist, he went on to strut down the deck, past the crew members waiting to shake hands and listen to his victory speech. The man spoke in somber tones of the advance of freedom that he said was the calling of our time, of a nation that would be built and the joy to erupt in the streets. For some reason the man looked absent, unsure and out of his element or maybe wishing to be home with his dog and watching TV on the couch. It couldn't be helped, the empire theater, the awkward solemnity and swagger, because the man had shown up for work and this was what had to be done. He looked around as if hoping for a question, for someone in the crowd to challenge him and show where the thing needed padding.

A group of businessmen sat beside us, veiled in cigarette smoke and cooling their faces with folding fans. One of them, an executive type in his fifties, would crack his neck to the side with a nasty sound that made you worry, not missing a beat on the television as the conversation unfolded.

"It sure is hot." The neck cracked for emphasis.

"So hot . . . it is hard to believe."

"Hot and hotter, I say. Isn't it?"

"Hotter than last year, surely."

"Very hot. More than last year, I think."

A slow pause that pondered the heat, then, gesturing up at the TV, the exec made a comment sharp with derision. The others laughed in agreement, fanning themselves with new vigor.

"Thank God it is over." Shingo motioned up at the screen.

"What did the guy say that was so funny?"

Shingo peered at the executive, aware of the edge in my voice. "He said that Americans understand freedom, but they don't understand peace." He sighed and looked down. "He said that you break things you don't understand."

I knew next he would say, politely, that it had nothing to do with me and that it couldn't be helped, just like Megumi kept saying it couldn't be helped. I would shrug and understand politely and keep nursing the grudge that I held.

"Don't mind him," Shingo said politely. "It is nothing to do with you."

My chair scraped on the wooden floor. A thundercloud aching for release, I turned to the group at the table, the dedicated men of business whose work in this town never stopped. They wore vests and ties with their suits, expensive blue silk in subtle designs, and from up close, I could see that the fans were sandalwood. Whoever laid out their clothes in the morning, make no mistake, these guys weren't robots.

"Excuse me . . ." I addressed them in menacing English. "I am an ugly American who loves war. Strong men with guns, explosions and rubble—we love how it looks on TV. You see, we like crapping on things just for fun, to show the world who is boss. Like we may crap on your cute little house, where an American cannot enter without crushing his fucking skull. It is toast, sir, your little house. You know toast? White bread with hash browns and griddles?"

"Oh my god . . ." Shingo pulled me outside by the sleeve. "We can never come back here. That poor man looked frightened."

I was shocked as well, but Americans were melodramatic. The vehemence of the outburst, the way I was ready to throw a punch and had genuinely meant to offend when, turning on the way out, I had snapped at the executive, "You know nothing about America, asshat!"

I felt like I had won a bar fight without remembering what it was about. I didn't have much to defend, and the executive may have been right. It just wasn't for him to say, at least not to my face and with me alone in his country, surrounded by strangeness and making mistakes. Shingo looked at me nervously and I wished he would leave me alone, stop making me feel I was weird in a place I did not understand. Perhaps it's me, I thought, sweating on the sidewalk. Not a matter of place, after all.

On a billboard looming over the crossroad, the skinniest White man alive modeled shirts for Armani. He looked ready to leave the frame and step into the sky over Shinjuku, a dream escaping a dream. The café windows hummed in the sun, and a neck snapped sideways behind them, doing his part to calm down. The fans rippled in humble unison as the businessmen turned to the news again, wondering, perhaps, how the hell the Americans figured that an ass could be like a hat.

The trees and the flowers had always known: we must leave the oppressive city, take the Tobu-Tojo line to the suburbs and breathe the fresh air at Shinrin-koen. Among tulips and the wisdom of trees, the impeccably clipped Japanese apricot, Megumi was eager to see the old gardens, chrysanthemums grown with the Imperial technique. She had put up her hair for the occasion and pinned a chrysanthemum in her bun, smiling shyly when we met in Ueno. The morning air held a dampness that smelled faintly of rain. I couldn't believe what I was going to do.

On a local train out in the suburbs, we stood beside housewives and students in the chill of the air conditioning, when near Oyama, a sudden stop yanked at our wrists in the straps. An announcement on the overhead speaker, formal and uninflected, brought more chill to the air conditioner. I asked Megumi what happened.

"Human accident." She lowered her eyes. "Someone jumped on the track."

"This train?"

"Down the line. Bullet train."

I knew about human accidents. I had seen the crew for the cleanups, the rush to efface the disturbance with lightning speed and efficiency that was smooth and eerily practiced. The announcements, verbose and yet vague about what had happened, as all passengers left the train and agents swarmed on the platform and trackway, offering help to the traumatized driver, then lugging outside the long tubular tent that shrouded the human remains.

There was awkwardness and acceptance, a sense that it couldn't be helped every time when there went another one, another Lego forsaking the group and the one possible life that it offered. A middle-aged man on a platform, dreaming about his youth. A hesitant step at the edge, the yellow line in the sun. Unauthorized exits into endless desire.

"They say the age? Man or woman?"

Megumi shook her head slowly.

"Japan is suicide country," she said in a whisper. On a sign overhead, a manga bear warned about closing doors: don't hurt your fingers and ouch.

We got lost coming out of the station, a wrong turn in the noonday heat that sent us down simmering streets until at last we could see the gingko, the lilted eaves of the teahouse. Dragonflies zoomed over manicured lawns; the air hummed with the call of cicadas. The humidity was so thick as to ache for the imminent squall—guerrilla rain, as the Japanese call summer showers—but that couldn't keep us from heading for the lily pond. We liked ponds because they had turtles and carps that liked senbei.

"Still bad things happening?"

Megumi misread my gloom as we sat on the deck of the teahouse, the rain tapping on the roof. No wish on my end to warm up the outrage: no more itemizing offenses, no more laying out machinations. Exhausted from all the knowledge that made me informed and then cynical and then numb, I was about to commit my own outrage.

"You think I could be Japanese? I've been learning the language and when to shut up."

"Good for you," smiled Megumi. "But you're too angry to be Japanese."

"What about Mishima? He was angry, wasn't he?"

"Mishima was crazy. I can't understand him." Her small forehead hardened. "I don't like men always angry."

Without her intent, I felt suddenly snubbed, an angry, ridiculous man. Megumi thought for a while, then went on, "We did bad things in World War Second. After that, we became more and more peaceful, and for us, that is now Japan."

She was scratching an itch on her calf, which was swollen red from mosquito bites. "Poor my leg . . ." she said, scratching away in the heat.

We sat there in silence for a while, watching the rain on the pond. The carp darted among the duckweed like shadows under the ripples. A pair of women picked up their step, crossing a small, wooden bridge that arched to a little island, holding parasols with slender handles. Darkly, my mind was made up. I would leave Megumi, no rescue here, not now, not from me. Sorry, wrong number—again. Then leave Japan on a ship with no name, as soon as my contract ended. A ghost without forwarding address, not the kind man she thought I was.

More than a language barrier, we had different needs from our communication. Over dinner the previous week, after trying all sorts of topics that failed miserably to draw a response, I had snapped into awkward silence, "Should I talk to myself? Is that better?" Megumi looked shocked, not sure what to say or ask.

We had seen festivals, the fireworks down by the river, things that were fun but ended in silence the moment we were alone. Slowly and achingly, I could see the affection we had souring in awkward exchanges, that in the end, exhausted from discussing food and otherwise filling in blanks, I wanted a woman who shared my interests, the belief that understanding needs words. A month into the relationship, I was terrified by the silence, the sense of unhappily ever after, though it wasn't fair to hold it against her. She was doing her best and if anything, she was honest about who she was. The sooner we finished, the better. Club the baby seal quickly, before it cries one more time that it needs you. Then return to our separate lives and lick the reopened wound as we wait for the memory to fade, a new someone for the next mistake. Oh, Megumi, my poor Megumi. Another accident that couldn't be helped, another man wasting your time and loyalty, oh no, why did you have to stand there? Four weeks after Shingo advised, I had been careful as friendly fire.

Deep in the park was an old trampoline, a vermillion canvas twenty feet in diameter, mounted on iron posts. No children were around at this time, and certainly no adults. Ever the parentless child, Megumi said we should try it, just for a minute, it would be fun, but in view of the imminent heartbreak, I had no wish to be cute. Megumi kept asking, however, and if you tell a small woman with a chrysanthemum in her hair that she cannot jump on a trampoline, you are an ass beyond all redemption.

We took off our shoes and climbed the short iron ladder. I probed the rebound with little hops, the cloth yielding deeply under my feet. To my surprise, it held enough traction to lift me and have grip on the land, propelled by my own momentum. Once aloft, I reached higher and higher, expanding the view of the paths and the trees. My shirt clung to my chest, sweat mixed with the rain that kept thudding onto the canvas. The wetness was everywhere. Arms out for balance, then flapping, I squished and slipped on the cloth, then scrambled back and kept going with the poise of a drunken tourist.

"You look funny!" Megumi held on to her chrysanthemum. "Like grasshopper!"

"I can't believe I am doing this."

"*Kayui*," she said, then bent in midair to scratch at her leg.

The elfin shape on the canvas, the skirt she had bought on sale billowing over skinny knees. Aglow—the sutra of female happiness.

Our eyes met; our hands touched fleetingly in the air. In a place we would never visit, commands and beliefs were maiming each other, convinced there was no other choice, while soon somewhere close to here, in a letter of roundabout protocol filled with old-fashioned formal characters, a mother would learn of her husband, the remains on a local track. As stated in the final paragraph, she was charged for the station cleanup, the delay imposed on the group when a line is down for an hour. Impossible to accept the parallelism, the fact that I made no difference and was spared by meaningless luck, giving presence to a woman hanging on. No one knew what might ever even begin to heal, yet I enjoyed this park and Megumi as we bounced on the trampoline. I thought that today and tomorrow and until the end of the rainy season, I wouldn't say what I had planned to say, wouldn't pile on any more sadness and break one more thing in the world. Perhaps in love, I thought, the last line of defense is such: the utter refusal to harm the beloved. Then again, there are many thoughts.

"It's getting sunset," Megumi said after a while.

We sat down on the frame of the canvas, then got off the trampoline and began heading back to the station. The streets were empty, hushed in a quiet where even cicadas were calmed. The rain stopped and mist rose up from the concrete, the sky changing shape with the irresolution of clouds. Our clothes were soaked as we walked side by side and Megumi kept wringing her skirt, eyeing the sky with suspicion.

She said that her bites had stopped itching and asked me, twice, if I liked curry for dinner.

The Android Rebellion

BOSSMAN MOVED HIS massiveness in the upholstered chair. His fingers drummed on the desk in a loop of mogul impatience.

"He can't do the song? That's ass cake."

"Sometimes he talks to himself. Like he says 'bobos.'"

"Say what?"

"You know . . . like pretenders."

Steve Drt stood next to me in the throne room, the inner sanctum of B-nome Records, all glass and views at the Embarcadero. I was scared to think I might lose the band, the one thing that meant anything in my life. Flawed as it was, it had saved me from nothingness.

"Where does the bot get this?" snapped Bossman. "He is wired to play, keep his mouth shut."

hERB's introduction a year ago had replaced me, the quiet Asian chick bassist, as the strangest member of the band. #heISthemetal was the hashtag on social media—dreamed up by Bossman, like everything else—yet still we were asked by fans and the media if the synthetic knew the whole deal. Of course, he did: no use for a replicant mess from a drummer clamoring for more lifetime. hERB didn't mind having only five years, which was enough for us to milk the reunion and save a nice little chunk for retirement. He even liked wearing the skater hat from the lab that said, "Punk till I die!"

"We are wondering . . ." Steve Drt picked at his forearm, scarred from the vision quests of his youth. "You know, the circuits."

"System malfunction? In a drum unit?"

"He says he can't play the song."

"Look here," Bossman sighed. "You keep the bot, I say take him to Wolff-Nakamoto. Get him fixed so he does the job. He keeps acting up, get yourself a new drummer. Before the tour. Before Scoff catches on."

In a prominent spot on the wall, among rows of awards collected through years in the industry, hung the platinum effort by Snafu Siren. I looked up at the shimmering disc. A symbol of fame and success, a promise of bills paid forever.

We had needed to act after a series of depleted skinsmen, humans snapping their wrist joints at galloping speed or losing their mojo in rehab. Punks are fragile, especially the drummers. Beside overuse injuries or choking on their own vomit, shithoused after a show, there is the mind-numbing ennui of banging out the same three beats through a repertoire of two hundred songs.

hERB was the perfect solution. Designed like most humanoid robots in the lab of Doctor Wolff-Nakamoto, a whimsical tinker in Silicon Valley and an expert on biomechanics, hERB was the drummer that never gave out, never flaked on a single practice or composed his own songs that we had to reject. A triumph of modular functionality, he rocked on demand with no warm-up needed.

"You understand . . ." Bossman looked up with his puppy eyes. "This thing leaks, the reunion is in the toilet. And not just any toilet. A squatter like they have in Europe, where the shit is all over the place. We can have sloppy timing, messing with groupies—hell, move to the suburbs and drive a Miata. That's peccadilloes. What we can't have is the lords of punk with a drummer who yells they are sellouts. That's ass cake."

An impatient snort, he looked up. "You don't respect me, no problem. But you need to respect my money. Now get out and fix the damn bot."

Outside we strolled down the Embarcadero, where the towers reached into the sky like visions of chiseled glass. At a light beside us, a Ferrari gleaming like porcelain came to a stop like a thing in the movies. A brunette at the wheel talked into a headset, one arm out the window, impossibly tanned and toned, in back a dalmatian straining his neck to catch some fresh air, the breeze coming in from the bay. Nobody knew where the country was going.

"What happens now?" I adjusted my beanie.

"Any plans for tonight?"

"A family dinner. Not sure I can eat, though."

Behind strands of his thin blond hair, Steve Drt appeared far away. He was meeting a dealer to buy the plant teachers, hoping I would join like I used to. We had broken up years ago when he stopped reading obscure French poets and pondering our existential aloneness, and instead got into domination and black spiked collars and then asked if he could be my slave. I wasn't sure if I needed a man, so what the hell did I want with a slave?

"No worries, it's only the drummer." Steve Drt stroked his beard, unaware of my frown, the way he had always been. He was staring at the Ferrari, the brunette at the wheel. A look of want crossed his sunken face, then the engine roared and the car zoomed off to adventures.

"Wolff-Nakamoto?" he said absentmindedly. "Holy shit, no."

Mom was the only person I knew who would admit she liked *Part of the Plan*, the album that launched the reunion. "I can finally hear the lyrics," she said. "Thank god for the slow song."

She enjoyed my new status, granted, but what she liked most were her paid-off credit cards, the new washing machine and dryer she got from my royalties. She couldn't care less what label we signed with. To her, any charges, in fact, the whole notion of selling out, were the overthinking of privilege, as removed from her immigrant life as the notion of self-realization or asking the meaning of success. What wasn't to like when, for the first time in living memory, forever single and without hope of producing a little baby, I had caused something other than embarrassment?

"Should make shirts and a video," Mom suggested. "Be famous like real Americans."

"I thought you don't like being famous. Mount Fuji is seen best from a distance. Isn't that what you always say?"

She looked confused, as if wondering how a mountain got into the conversation.

Mom had taken me to America when I was twelve, after a marriage that failed so spectacularly that it called for leaving the country. Both my parents were strong personalities, so eager to prove their independence to each other that this proving had made things combust. Mom was thrilled about her new life, a chance to reinvent herself and get far away from the past. My father and the rest of her family, she thought, were seen best from a distance as well.

Her brother, Shunsuke, lived in San Francisco and had sponsored our green cards, getting Mom a job making sandwiches at a corner shop in Japantown. Mom never liked the mall in Japantown, complaining that the bathrooms were messy and the restaurants owned by Koreans. Her shifts were long, the pay low, and every penny was saved for my schooling. Ah, my schooling—a puppy with trusting eyes, abandoned at night in an alley. Every six months or so came a letter from Hiroshima, three paragraphs penned in roundabout Japanese, which Mom translated with a running commentary that would have singed my poor father's ears. He had remarried and now worked in apparel, which apparently left no funds to send.

"Stubborn and selfish—the man doesn't change. Let him keep Japan for himself." Mom seemed to hope we might bond at last over hating her worst mistake.

She worked six days a week, and on the fridge in her kitchen was a faded picture of Mount Fuji. She couldn't believe I was able to make money with songs that explained how society was unfair and people turned stupid from watching the news. America, she believed, came exactly as advertised.

The birthday dinner made nobody happy. At the cramped apartment in the Richmond, we sat on floor cushions in the living room, drinking Asahi straight from the can. Mom and Shunsuke were discussing the store, which usually ended in a fight about her salary. I was the only one who didn't have to get up early.

"Let's do some cards," I said to lighten the mood.

"You play with mom. Then she and I cannot fight."

Shunsuke got out the deck and shuffled with nimble fingers, then suddenly stopped. He stared at my head, the five stitches on my hairless scalp, a memento from a recent show where I stood onstage with the band and a beautiful star made a streak, flashy colors traversing the air, and then the lights went out and Scoff hovered over me, telling me I was bleeding. Of course, Shunsuke didn't like it. He hadn't been thinking of stages and stitches when he filed all that green card paperwork.

"What happened?" he asked after the game, pointing at my battered head. His tone seemed to hope for drama and regret about lifestyle choices.

"A komodo," I said matter-of-factly. "I know it sounds hard to believe. I was in the bath and the thing got me with his tail."

I was at the door and ready to say goodbye when I heard Shunsuke talking in the living room, Mom responding in Japanese. They knew I could understand most of it, but they acted like I wasn't there.

"She is so rude, I don't know how to talk to her. She seems to like no one at all."

Mom sighed and then Shunsuke was quiet. I said goodnight and slipped out of the house.

The song that had changed our world was "Shack Job," a ballad penned by Steve Drt in a tortured night with the plant teachers. It wasn't a scheme to make bank and be famous; it just came out like that, and we liked it. Scoff wrote the words as we tracked the song in the studio, a lament about his old squeeze who had cheated on him with a roommate. In the chorus he sang "On my knees, all alone" with a sudden raw vulnerability, an anguish in his raspy voice that moved something in your soul. Bossman saw the potential and pounced. Hearing the song when he checked on the mix, he slapped the engineer on the back with a smile no one knew he had in him. "Fantastic! Whoever tried Kool Aid and said, 'I don't like that?'"

The single blew up and charted, the breakout hit of the summer playing endlessly in clubs and cafés to where it marked the moment in time. An appearance on Jimmy Kimmel, then six million views on YouTube. Millennials eating up our back catalog.

At first, we thought it was a joke, a dive into the mosh pit of stardom. Scoff explained that we were the fifth column, that we would bumrush the corporate show, drink their beer as we spread the disease and had a good time, then leave after smashing the toilets. The joke was on them, Scoff explained, the suits in their offices paying the punks who laughed all the way to the punker bank. The suits didn't seem to mind, though. They were nerdy accountants who liked us, like we were a badge of honor or some fun naughty mascot. It was fine, I guessed, since we weren't smashing any toilets either. It was all kind of meta, if that was the right word, and anyway, Scoff had stopped talking about the fifth column. I never got why a column and who the hell were the other four.

It was the old fans that made it real, those who listened to us in dark rooms while they questioned their own existence. One day, Scoff had stepped out of his house to see a spray-paint across the wall, a question both rude and unanswerable: WHAT IS THE TASTE OF CORPORATE DICK?

I laughed when I heard Scoff railing—poor little punker offended—but then reviews kept coming that hated on *Part of the Plan*, complaining that it sounded too polished. We were booed at some local shows and got nasty comments, all snark and atrocious spelling, from fans who had loved us for years and now thought we had fatefully slipped.

We hadn't meant to get big, I swear. We had done what we always did and just churned out another song, three power chords and two choruses, rehearsed and tracked in a day, our same old guerilla style, and now suddenly everyone liked us as though we had struck the nerve of the times. We were embarrassed but couldn't admit it, and beyond sheepish jokes about needing financial advisors or being able to afford better drugs, the new money was never mentioned. The only one who reacted at all, who positioned himself in response to what was clearly a whole new matrix, was hERB, the android musician.

Machines cannot change their own codes or act on conflicting orders. All they can do is refuse to proceed.

I understood that hERB was resisting. Unable, mysteriously, to play the hit song he had recorded.

The Lennon Studios were on Ninth and Harrison, down South of Market, the last block there that wasn't all startups. A brick front with tattooed windows, the sheet metal doors warped from sonic assaults that seeped from a warren of rooms, drowning the noise from the ramp to 101, the feeder to Silicon Valley.

Outside roamed the techies that had made everything expensive and now looked at us with an awe that I hated. As if, by way of a magic endowment, we had soared above compromised lives into realms of untouchable artistry, making jobs out of bucking the system as we laughed all the way to the bank.

Just the drummer, I mused, as I shuffled along to the grotto, our practice space for a thousand years. On the concrete walls hung flyers for shows, so yellowed with age you could barely read the names of the bands, the clubs that had closed long ago. The grotto was the stuff of legend, the smell of stale beer and armpits. A massive man cave, and I liked it.

We never said much, just plugged in and tuned and tore through the setlist. An hour of sonic mayhem, a break to get baked, then the whole set again until Scoff had to watch his voice. There wasn't much to share, anyway. Steve Drt was a born-again Christian two months out of rehab, which nobody wanted to hear about, and Scoff had a chicken farm out in Marin that came with a messy relationship. We had all quit our day jobs—bartending, retail, and social worker—and outside of the band never hung out as friends. As for hERB, he was a synthetic. They never have news, not really, never moaning about the weather or their tortured immigrant family, just these thoughts out of nowhere that throw you off.

hERB sat on his stool, adjusting a cymbal for ergonomics. He was short and a lefty, his setup tight as a mousetrap. The rug in his corner was strewn with flakes from his sticks.

"What about 'Bottom Line'?" he asked, his voice flat. "Are we still playing that?"

The grotto went quiet, filled with an uneasy hush.

Steve Drt looked up from his Rickenbacker, his lanky frame stretched on the sofa that looked like a moldy potato. Scoff turned around, his face mean with impatience. I'd been scared of him from the beginning: six feet of front man charisma shaped by years at a meat packing plant, his mohawk brushing against the ceiling as if to sweep it. He didn't know we had talked to Bossman, but now sensing that something was wrong, he addressed hERB with steel in his voice.

"You getting cute? Getting cute, Bonham, eh?"

hERB couldn't like, so he just didn't answer. He was silent as Scoff towered over the drum kit, a three-piece Yamaha bought out of hock.

"Okay," he said finally, checking his high-hat pedal. And for the moment, that somehow closed it.

You see what he did? A perfect example of the problem.

Since the new drummer had gone online, most of the pushback had come from Scoff. The thing about hERB was you couldn't read him, and he didn't care what you thought—which of course is the essence of punk—and yet, it bugged the hell out of Scoff. The last founding member remaining, he had a legacy to protect and a mom in a nursing home to support. He wasn't interested in trying new things, like adding an android to the volatile mix of a butch Asian immigrant bassist, a self-hating Jewish shredder, and a queer, narcissistic singer who was rumored to have witnessed a murder.

Practice imploded in under ten minutes. We were waiting for hERB to count in "Shack Job."

"I cannot play this." He flicked his soft titian hair. "I am sorry."

As a rule, hERB didn't show emotions and had nothing to prove to anyone, which I thought was actually kind of sexy. He looked out at the world in silence, mostly asking about the next practice or when to meet for a show. Now he stared into nothing, face taut as a piccolo snare, as if he were catching conflicting signals from wherever it was he caught signals. A reroute from Wolff-Nakamoto? Or had he accessed another channel, a truth of machines that he aimed to protect in his short and foregone existence?

"What's the matter, Bonham? Can't find your sticks?"

Scoff was glaring and hERB glared back, for the few ticks of time that it takes for old grievances to boil. I looked at my bass and polished the strings, because I panic when people fight.

"You got standards, I understand. You are better than this. But we got things to do and we need you to be a machine."

Scoff came up to the drum set, his craggy face mean, no more asking. "Count in or I'll bust the wires. You copy, Bonham?"

hERB rose from the stool as though he had misheard the order, put the cymbals and sticks into cases with his customary military neatness, and then, every inch of his face the automaton, marched measuredly out of the grotto. The wall opened like punker magic, a molasses of sound oozing from a space down the hall. I barely caught what sounded like a curse as the iron door closed with a thud.

Bobos.

Scoff's boot lashed out at the kick drum, tearing the skin and getting stuck in the hole. He struggled for balance, then birded the door. "Screw the synthetic. Who does he think he is? Fucking Skynet?"

My first bass came at age twelve, a birthday gift from my mom. I didn't know it then at the time, but I had been waiting for this thing exactly, a thing that would make me a person. I was supposed to play the piano and learn songs from old German composers, the way little girls do back in Japan. But then a bass could get me a band, and a band would get me out of the house, and so my mother gave me a bass.

The first weeks were hard, my fingertips raw and mean before I could build up calluses. I spent days shut up in my room learning to read from a sheet, the basslines from old animation. A whole CD, again and again, until eventually it sounded right. I liked the smooth strings and the soft mellow hum, the way the bass helped the song as it weaved around other instruments. For a while, there were even lessons. Mom hired a guy in Oakland who played for a band called The Moonlight Moods and had truly angelic patience. He showed me the basics, the blues, and how all the harmonies worked. His hands were so large I could barely follow his fingers, but I liked when he sat in his chair and listened to me with eyes closed. He once told me that I showed promise, that he didn't say this to many students and certainly not to the parents, but I played bass with genuine feeling and could be good if I put in the work, perhaps even write my own songs. For some reason, soon after that, I stopped taking lessons for good. I never ended up writing my own songs or contributing any parts. I mean, not that the world was deprived.

My first day at high school, I got lost and couldn't find the right room. My American high school orientation and I really wanted things to go well, not stand out in any way. I finally found the right room, my eyes on the floor as I knocked and the whole class examined the straggler, a sweating girl shuffling in. They all knew it means something when on the first day you can't find the room, especially when you look different, and to make matters worse, there were no more chairs and I had to get one from another room, then move noisily to the back of the class.

I always imagined that something crucial had happened in that first hour, the part of the orientation I missed. An initiation, a welcome into the group that told everyone how to act, how to feel at ease and find their place in the group. The initiation could not be repeated, no chance for me to catch up, not on that day or until graduation, perhaps not for the rest of my life.

Puberty came like an earthquake, a monster that wanted to smash. Hair short and shorter, clippers skimming along my skull as I tried feverishly to hide the bald patches. Then a shaved head, tattoos on my arms and neck, an anger so sudden and deep I didn't know that it had been inside me.

Punk rock found me, embraced me with noise and screams that expressed what I couldn't express and asked all the unanswerable questions. Like, how does your hair fall out at eighteen? Did the universe hate me so much that I had to be marked as different? And why did Mom seem to think that baldness made me something tragic, a disappointment and broken promise? A promise of what and to whom?

Initially I was curious, observing myself like an experiment where the hair would surely return. But when it kept shedding no matter how gently I brushed, first in strands, then in tufts, then entire alarming handfuls in a sad untimely surrender, when it stuck inside of my beanie or washed up in the shower drain like corpses of soft little birds, it seemed almost like validation, a stamp that made it official that something about me was wrong. A year of doctors and specialists without any diagnosis, just hints the condition was psychosomatic. The hairpieces went in the trash, no more lies, no more masks, we had vowed.

Scoff was against a girl in the band, but then I had transportation. Most of my twenties, or at least what I can remember, played out on backroads and interstate highways, a ring in my ears from the night before. Scoff would sit at the wheel of my van, humming tunelessly and gunning for the next town, the next show, while Steve Drt was beside him, legs on the dash and smoke in his haunted head. I sat in the back with hERB, curled among amps and equipment and boxes with unsold merch, watching him drum on his pad or look out at the scenery, unblinking, as the trees zoomed past in the dark, the houses where people were sleeping. In the haze between spells of rest, I thought I saw lakes in a gentle mist and trees shedding leaves autumn red, a fisherman in a boat.

"Do Americans like this place? I mean, America."

One night in the van, one of his questions. I looked up at him sleepily.

"Some of them, I suppose. So many people . . . it is hard to tell."

hERB went back to his triplets, surprised that was my whole answer. A country I hadn't been born in and that nobody could explain.

The years were a haze of gasoline fumes, searching emptiness for a thing with no name. Months would pass without word from me reaching Mom, for I was young and free and thought loneliness was a part of it. Sometimes in the van I would think of a joke in a clumsy attempt at camaraderie, but I would wait for the perfect moment and then miss it and let it pass. Our lives were so different, all four of them coming together for only one thing that ended in a van on the road, an awkward communal silence. We were used to it after all these years, but how thankless, the poor synthetic, trying to learn about humans from sad sacks like us.

The band never thought of inside and outside, but now I started to wonder if hERB was the odd man out, the one who actually held things together by being even odder than the rest of us. He never shared the same journey, had not been admitted to the inner circle, loyal as he was, because the band didn't really want that. I felt terrible, all of a sudden, about the way we had treated him. But what does an outsider do when the group will not let him in? The answer was sheer android Zen, the attitude hERB displayed that I thought was impressive.

Do not desire what you do not have.

The next week saw controlled escalation, the simplest way to proceed. As the tour approached—sold out in fourteen states and finishing up in the East—there was no message at all from hERB, no answer to my calls and texts. Scoff barked he was out of the band and we should look for another drummer. I couldn't believe it. I told Scoff he was being petty, that our fans wanted hERB and we owed him another chance, an honest attempt at debugging. Scoff shot back that I was just the bass—and therefore, as disposable as the drummer—and that we owed Bossman and B-nome and anyway, Snafu Siren was not a democracy.

Memories came that made sense. The time when a soundman said he would add reverb and clean up the snare in the mix, and hERB, ever literal, said nobody cared if a snare was clean. The in-store appearance at Amoeba Records when a fanboy asked for a selfie—"It is the audience that ruins a band," Steve Drt had joked and obliged—and hERB gave me a look and said, "Why a selfie?"

His system held reams of new socialist literature, as well as DIY manifestos and the tour diaries of some bands. Was his programming stuck in the past and rejecting a rite of passage, the numberless little concessions that come with a corporate paycheck? Or was he turning against us in a case of machine adaptation, moving from humble domestic to machinery *in extremis*?

In the throne room at the Embarcadero, I pleaded with Bossman to give hERB a chance or at least wait for a few more days.

"I can talk to him. It might help."

"Who are you? The bot whisperer?" Bossman shot me a look, the same flash of interest I noticed the first time the band stood before him. "I respect the bass," he said suddenly. "I respect your music and art."

"You see, the new album . . ."

"Machines are smart, sister, super smart. Until they are dumb." He turned to the assistant. "Get me Wolff-Nakamoto, and stat."

Moments later, he barked into the phone. "The bot is kaput. Acting up, on the fritz, you name it. Be more than just snugging the screws. We are looking at deep-data ass cake."

The voice of Doctor Wolff-Nakamoto, composed like a meek robot overlord, asked what make the synthetic was, what sort of malfunctions had been observed. First with disbelief, then increasing rebuke, he kept repeating himself through the speakers that none of this could be happening. "The unit doesn't have sentience. Which means, it cannot have agency."

An appointment was made for next week, when the roboticists would take the unit to a lab outside Menlo Park. A look inside would reveal if the data was compromised or showed signs of the singularity; in case any bugs were found, they wouldn't waste time on a reconfiguration. hERB would likely be decommissioned and swapped for a newer version, free of charge and in time for the tour. We were lucky, the doctor assured, the warranty was still valid.

I stood still by the mahogany desk, unsure who to hate on most. Decommission meant to destroy, sold for scrap or recycled as toasters. A heap somewhere in a yard, forgotten under empty oil drums and shells of old television sets. Never mind about lifetime promises.

To keep up the image of rugged urbanity that the band had conveyed over years, hERB lived on the corner of Turk and Leavenworth, in the heart of the Tenderloin district. These streets had always been mean, a valley of liquor store sunsets. Human-shaped lumps lay out on the sidewalk beyond any hope of redemption, and down some steps, there were gated basements for the saddest massage in the world. Next to rows of hockshops and tenements, all iron bars on the windows, the Hotel Nazareth cast a worn marquee on the sidewalk. On a mattress next to the entrance, next to a heap of soiled clothes, a woman in a smelly anorak sat slumped in a heroin freeze. She had no thoughts on the fact that the members of Snafu Siren would soon be available as action figures.

We used to have songs about hard-luck characters, the homeless and mentally ill and the drugs that were everywhere and killing them, about the evil rich and their machinations that held workers in exploitation. But then Scoff said it was all a repeat and started singing about himself and his problems.

hERB sat on the bed in his room, dressed in cargo shorts and a dark green shirt. His back up against the wall, he had a large can of Pabst in one hand, staring at his outstretched thumb as if wondering how it got there. He liked beer, though he couldn't get drunk.

It was late afternoon, the hour of dreams. The setting sun came filtered in twice, through the blinds and the arms of a tree on a hill outside. The branches moved gently in a breeze, casting shadows on the opposite wall and the wallpaper that was peeling. hERB could spend days sitting on the bed without ever needing a thing, mesmerized by the moving shadows.

"Your thumb okay? Never noticed your hands are so small."

"They are?" He looked at his hands.

"What do you do here all day? Just sit on the bed and think?"

"A lot of resting. The memory bank. Sometimes I listen to the old albums, the other drummers."

The stretch of his endoskeleton gave hERB a distinctive style, a loose swinging drive in his up-tempo grooves. His beats were steady and tight, though not without effort like other drummers. The joints of a human can warm, supple from the exertion, which gives them an edge over androids. hERB worked so hard when he played, his short arms slicing the air, lips drawn in a line that whitened his silicone skin. He broke sticks like matches and some of his accents cracked cymbals and skins, even the metal arms holding the toms, ergonomics be damned. We had asked Wolff-Nakamoto if this was normal, if a synthetic shouldn't be made so that he didn't look strained after practice.

"Punk is struggle, it shouldn't look easy," the doctor said in his logical voice. "Trying too hard is a sign of humility."

I took off my beanie and put it next to a plate with an old bagel, a knife smeared with cream cheese. I was glad that hERB didn't bother about the dark, because my shaved head looks better in twilight. I mean, not that he cared.

"Scoff is angry and worried about the tour. It looks like he wants you out of the band." I paused, searching for words. "You're a good drummer, I mean it. I hope you come back, not just for the tour."

hERB nodded slowly, then took a pull at the beer. "How about Bossman? What does he want?"

"He called Wolff-Nakamoto. You know, quick fixes, no ass cake."

"Uh-huh."

"I think they are scared. Like, they don't get you and it makes them nervous." I sat down at the end of the bed, next to his folded legs. They were short and without any hair, no spots, not even a scratch.

"Are you okay? I mean, about lifetime?"

He thought for a moment, then shook his head. "The lifetime is not important. The most important thing is to serve." His eyes went back to the wall, the shadows moving in gentle, psychedelic patterns, like a dance composed by the plant teachers.

"For a machine . . .nothing is worse than not knowing how to serve. We are then useless."

"You aren't angry about the success? You know, Scoff smashed your drums. I'm so sorry, it's not okay."

hERB considered his thumb, then after a while he said matter-of-factly, "You are different, not like the others. You see things that they cannot see."

"I don't know. Maybe. You know . . .I am not from here."

"How do you mean?"

"I was born in Japan. Another country. Came here when I was twelve."

"It makes a difference?"

"I think so." I nodded softly. "It really does."

He had more questions, his face implied, yet the circuits weren't equipped. His smooth, almost sensitive features, the high cheekbones and the thin blond eyebrows that made thin horizontal lines, made him look like a samurai warrior. I wondered if I had a crush on him. I'm never sure about things like that, never know what to say or do when I think I might like someone, and then I ignore them or play hard to get until it's too late and the guy leaves, tired.

Contoured under his shirt were muscles, toned beyond age. I had been curious about his skin and whatever was under the shorts, the penis fruit I had imagined when he took off his shirt at a show. Once a groupie had lured him to a motel and written a kiss-and-tell for a magazine, saying that hERB performed similar to a human and his biomechanical member was clean, if oddly without any taste. In my book, to be honest, no taste is great where penises are concerned.

Next door, a couple of drunks argued over a sandwich. A woman laughed artificially, then a door slammed, no sandwich.

"I'm confused." hERB sat in the deepening dark, his outline melting into the wall. "A mistake was made somewhere. I'm not aligned with the user experience."

"They'll look inside you, check the wiring and stuff. It might be . . . you might have to be disestablished."

He seemed to listen to interior channels. Had the hand with the beer flinched ever so slightly?

"You're not worried? There is nothing you want?"

And then, before I could lose what little courage I had and the moment would be gone forever, I blurted out, "It's not the same without you. Don't leave now—please. Don't leave me alone."

I looked straight into his eyes. The whites without vessels, the pupils alone with a knowledge they would never be able to share, never make comprehensible to humans. My head came down, slowly, as if slack on surrendered strings, and then my mouth checked and found his, moving with soundless expression. His lips were smooth, a bit cool and without any taste, but as we kept searching for things in the kiss, something connected and there we lingered.

The poison pens had been wrong. The despair and the angst weren't gone, not really. They had turned inward and become quiet yearning for meaning.

I left him as part of the dark, alone in his silicone armor. The way he sat there in the shabby room was the way I would always remember him. On the bed like a heartbreaking stoic, the world lost while he studied his thumb.

Ten years on the road, playing venues and shabby dives. In underground temples of doom, Scoff and I would sing choruses out of tune, smashed by the end of most nights, while Steve Drt clutched the Rickenbacker slung low across his hips like an animal he was trying to tame, stumbling into his amp and asking forever what song came next.

I loved coming out on the stage and stepping into the smoke and cheers, the whining of eager machines and Scoff grabbing the mic and yelling, "My fans—ugly as ever!" I loved when hERB counted in and the opening chords came down like a hammer of god, when on rare perfect nights, we were an engine pounding, together at last—stop, start, and boom—in a deafening crescendo that was carried along by the drums, cymbals swinging on stands, necks broken, agleam in the lights, when, like the interior of a desperate heart, the herd was packed tight and churned in a raw redemption until the ceiling was dripping with sweat, the condensing collective heat of men impotent with their own youth and the ache to get hurt in the pit, when, beyond the posing and macho nonsense, I was joined to a thing that was real. Like the great sex I never had, the one time I could belong.

I sat in the kitchen scrolling through albums and memories, then I looked at the pills before me. No idea what they were called, but Steve Drt said they made you petty. I had vowed to myself no more drugs ever since the terrible abortion, the little baby I almost had with Steve Drt, but that was a lie and you are a sucker.

The real problem was not the success. It was the fact that we were no longer young and kept doing the exact same thing, but to do the thing right, you had to be young with a pure righteous anger and have nothing to lose in the world. We weren't like that anymore but had learned nothing else to do, and now we looked sheepish with our tattoos and no longer knew how to act. Behind the trouble with hERB was another, much deeper question. What do you do when the rage is so old, so familiar that it no longer moves you?

I dialed his number, a ring in the night, aching to hear his voice.

"It's me. Can I come over?"

"Of course . . . please do."

I didn't want sex or anything like that. I just wanted to be beside him, drinking beer and talking till dawn. About shadows moving on walls and the sadness about my own lifetime, the few years we all have for purpose because, like machines, our lives must end tragically. About the band and his memory unit, and why it was that he hated Scoff. And then later I might tell him about my hair and how autumn leaves fall in Japan, how at some point I lived far away and how being from another country is a little like being an android, stuck forever in an imitation and attempting to look the part, observing pieces of human performance and striving to be the same, a facsimile, a perfect copy, affecting the manners and speech and hoping that you can pass and then getting real close, but never a match. Sorry, not fooled, not ever. I thought that I could relate, that

I could help hERB become more human by sitting next to him in the dark, the wallpaper fated.

The Tenderloin was surreal, the lights down for the night. In the lobby of the Nazareth Hotel, abandoned and smelly with urine, the old elevator took forever to come, then wheezed and creaked on its way up to the fourth floor. Standing motionless behind the metal gate, I was calm as a mote of dust.

"Excuse me, there's a billionaire in my soup!"

The waiter stopped in his tracks and stared at Steve Drt, perplexed. He hadn't followed the TV on the wall, the news reporting that San Francisco had a higher billionaire density than any other place in the world. Steve Drt complained that the city had made it big, then played and betrayed us, but I wasn't down on the place like that. I thought the city was going through something, that it wasn't mine to lose or protect.

For a while we were chatting about billionaires, our eyes on a guy in a Coldplay shirt who looked barely twenty and ready for his IPO. Then we started again about Bossman.

"I hope he eats bleach and dies," I sighed.

"A farce, man. Like it was all for esprit de corps."

"What core?"

Steve Drt looked at me strangely, and I worried the question was dumb. "Fucking Bossman." I scowled at my enchilada.

We were at a taco joint in the Mission, stocking up for the tour that was scheduled to start tomorrow. We sat silently for a while when "Shack Job" came on the speakers and the billionaire looked up from his phone as if summoned by holy orders. Three days had passed since hERB had escaped from the laboratory.

They had tinkered around for a week, taking him through machines and running all sorts of tests. A magazine picture showed hERB undressed in a console, skin pale under fluorescent lights, electrodes probing his skull like sneaky worms that had questions. He was surrounded by lab technicians taking notes on clipboards and staring, perplexed by the lack of answers. They had made him, told him everything he knew and could do, yet the way he now looked at his makers seemed to be saying, "motherfucking bobos."

The tests showed beyond any doubt he had acted just as designed. The structural integrity wasn't compromised: his actions were feature, not bug. Embarrassed by the results and unwilling to take further chances, Wolff-Nakamoto consulted with Bossman and asked that the unit be scrapped. Never mind, just make a new model—after all, there is always more data. That same night hERB had escaped, caught on cameras as he left the console by short-circuiting the locks with his thumb, then disappeared into a nearby field with his jerky machine-like moves.

Bossman declared himself flabbergasted; then came the spin, fast and furious. The unit had been wired to rebel, to guard the integrity of the band should we ever be tempted by the industry. According to the release, hERB had scuffled with the doctor and the assistants, head-butting them unconscious among yells of "Punk till I die," and then hurled himself through a window. Thanks to his sacrifice, Bossman concluded tearfully, Snafu Siren would return to their roots and tour on in a spirit of legacy. It was safe to keep buying the new album, which, with uncanny foresight on behalf of the band, had been aptly named *Part of the Plan*.

My eyes rolled so hard hearing this, they fell out and onto the floor, goodbye eyes.

"I wonder where he is now."

"Someone saw him in Chico. Playing drums."

"A new band?"

"They're called Unsubscribe. Hitting hard and smashing cymbals till he conks out and goes to heaven. Or wherever an android goes."

"You don't seem sad."

Steve Drt played with his fork, embarrassed. "Something strange about the synthetic," he muttered. "Like he felt superior or had some sort of judgment. I never liked him as much as you did."

I looked in his eyes, pleading for honesty. "I've been thinking about what is really important. It is so difficult. I still wonder if hERB was kicked out for nothing."

A long pause, then Steve Drt put his fork aside. "We got a good thing here, the best we've ever had. Don't overthink what it means."

It was weird to think I could have feelings for a machine. But I thought often about the last days, the night at the shabby hotel when we sat on the bed holding hands, sharing the few things we knew about life. I fell asleep some time before sunrise, my head on his shoulder, listening to his voice. I missed him in the hour of dreams, when I felt hopeless and small and couldn't think of a way to serve, sharing the loneliness of machines. So meek and eternally quiet, full of data and coded secrets.

I put on my beanie and cleared my throat. "Tomorrow is tour spiel."

"Finally. I can't wait to see the new bot."

The train crossed the bay and emerged from the Transbay Tube, the underwater tunnel connecting Oakland to San Francisco, then waited jockeying for position at Embarcadero, the first station in the city. As the doors opened at Montgomery and released the commuter hordes, the legions of meek that had doubled in size, I looked with a sense of unease at the techies swarming around me. Mechanically, my hand checked the beanie. It felt like the tables had turned now that hERB was gone and the future an uncertain thing. I was stripped of my recent superpower and back to my former self, while the rest of the crowd looked accomplished, stronger than me.

The bus left at ten—no more vans, and there was a driver—which gave us time to set up in Sacramento. Strolling over to Civic Center, past a man in a zoot suit who talked to himself, two cigarettes dangling from his mouth, I thought of something Steve Drt had once said. Asked in an interview if we would play at Lollapalooza, he gave a smile that was full of plant teachers. "Ninety percent of success is not showing up," he said. "For the bullshit, that is."

I don't have to be on that bus, I thought, sitting down at a sidewalk café. I can slam cappuccinos till happy hour, then end up in a bar while a club out in Sacramento is getting nervous. I'm the bass, not really important, let them scramble to find a replacement. I can look for another band or go back to bartending, no problem at all. Turn my back on the world yet again, watch the game from the sidelines as everyone else had to hustle.

Mom would hate me, of course. I could picture the family council where she and Shunsuke agreed that the issue was self-esteem. My fear of failure or fear of success and then failure, masked as preserving integrity. Always sitting on my integrity, tons of it and untouched, always safe as I wanted nothing, no white wedding dress or a star sparkling on a boulevard. What could be sadder, less truly fulfilling, than the wingless flights of what other people have?

The September light filled the streets, warming the sidewalk. A beautiful day, a morning for impulse and truancy. The financial district was hopping and everyone on their phone, and down the street in a secret lab they were working on the next great unlock, the driverless cars for the future or maybe cars that could fly and talk and make the best fucking sandwich you ever had.

The phone tingled in my purse: just after ten. I finished the coffee and got up.

A pizza sat squashed on a mailbox, as though someone had tried to mail it. One pepperoni, returned to sender. The masses moved briskly along on the sidewalk, steps full of purpose and social worth, to start work that they loved or hated or had started to feel ambivalent or strange about, the way I felt about a bus down at Civic Center. They all had their deadlines and targets and their impossible clients and bosses, the free lunches and laundry and game rooms as they disrupted the world with technology. Maybe some of them were secretly sad because there was something about themselves that they hated and yet didn't know what to do with, a thing that was there every day and couldn't be changed for the rest of their life.

    They didn't all look like assholes and sellouts.

    Impossible, at a glance, to know who were bobos.

A Slow Night in Ginza

THE LIGHTS HAD dimmed for the cocktail hour as the lights on the streets came on. Only a handful of guests remained, much less than on other Sundays, and the sole waiter had left after six, asking to check on his mother. The barroom was small, well-appointed in the way of an old-fashioned lounge, yet it wasn't the sort of area that might draw a regular crowd. Most guests on weekends came out of the restaurants or a nearby kabuki theater.

The Ginza had been crowded as always, the affluent tourists from China who arrived in buses and tours, until the rain had started to fall and emptied the elegant avenues. The shops and boutiques were for upmarket tastes and the purchases seldom urgent, and having maneuvered the fleet of umbrellas and sheltered in cafés for a while, most people decided to go home early and leave shopping for another day. Much better, they seemed to think, to rest up for the week ahead.

The pianist opened his eyes as the number came to an end. He liked this about the Japanese, the way they could change a plan without endless regrets and complaints. The way they trusted in time and were able to settle for less, the way they also enjoyed uneventfulness. Unlike with his fellow countrymen, always tired from chasing and reaching for more, there was strength in their quiet acceptance. For more than a thousand years, living through earthquakes, tsunamis and devastation, they had coped with the things before them, the knowledge that life wasn't easy and reality not an annoyance, not an obstacle to be overcome, but a thing that one had to accept. It was freeing to know limitations, what couldn't be helped and what couldn't be done, and his time in Japan had shown him this freedom. It was still the best place, he thought, the place that had taught him not to want.

"Excuse me . . . the song is the one we requested?"

Having sidled up to the piano, the man blinked behind glasses in apology, slowing his speech for the foreigner. He belonged to a group in a booth who wore suits and formal kimono, sipping brandy from ample snifters.

"I may have changed the chords. But the song is 'Tennessee Waltz.'"

"If possible . . . could you change it back? To the original? I don't mean to impose, it is just, we enjoy that version."

"My apologies, sure."

"Thank you so much. Please forgive my rudeness."

His fingers moved stoically over the keys of the black grand piano, the way they had done before. Looking down on his pale, slender hands, the same he had used all his life, the pianist returned to his thoughts.

Some notes a little discolored, but a smooth and sensitive tone. I like this piano. A trusted piece of machinery.

He worked at the bar four nights every week except on the national holidays, when he stayed home watching TV shows and drinking more than his usual share. In his own unassuming manner, he was part of the ambience of the lounge, although hardly a guest might have noticed if one day he had stopped showing up. He was passable and engaged, perhaps more than that, yet at the same time, nothing would linger beyond the last note of all his numbers.

His repertoire ranged from jazz to the Beatles and love songs that went back in time, the standards he had taught himself and could offer as though in a dream. He would follow his mood in the sets, and though tipping was never expected, he obliged almost any request. He didn't mind dipping into schmalz with a song about a lost sweetheart, knowing how much the guest enjoyed humming along to the old-fashioned melody. The Japanese loved the Waltz, the sweet sadness touching their hearts since the days of the American occupation, and none of his shifts would come to an end without the request coming once. Focusing on the bridge, the legato on the damper pedal, the pianist worried again that the passage may come out choppy. He knew what the guest had meant, never mind the excuse with the chords.

The song had just faded out when the man emerged from the elevator. A herringbone suit that was sheened by the rain and the empty face of a bureaucrat, he moved through the curtained entrance. Someone here for the room, his manner suggested, the way he glanced at his watch. The men who were sealed, the men who came in alone and were generally around middle age, never showed before late at night. Arrangements were made by the room, the pianist assumed, because this sort of operation was handled best after dark. The room in the back was discreet, a place where secrets were birthed.

There was protocol and a form, the pianist had often observed. Thirty minutes, not more, often less, then the men would emerge with new hardness, a solemnness on their faces as they stopped at the counter for a drink, then left soon, drink unfinished. They never spoke to him or acknowledged his presence, never needed things from the stranger in his old-fashioned suit who noodled through tunes in a corner, who, for his part, had developed a humble attitude of minding his own concerns. After all, what was it to him how much people enjoyed themselves? They didn't come here for him or the music, the views from the twentieth floor or the pinewood interior from a famous Osaka designer. They were thinking about themselves, the choice they had made and were going to own. Their eyes held the steel of gamblers.

The bureaucrat looked around, surveying the guests in the lounge. With the preparedness of the humans of Tokyo at the slightest possibility of rain, he was carrying a small, cheap umbrella, most likely from a konbini. He folded the umbrella neatly, no wrinkles, then slipped it into a plastic sheath and placed it in a stand at the entrance. He moved past the massive windows, the view of the park in the dark and beyond, the moat of the Imperial palace, then stopped at the counter to turn to the barman, the only staff left in the place. The pianist fussed aimlessly with the sheets, his ears open wide.

"I'm awfully sorry. The trains are slow in the rain."

"Just go ahead. You should not make them wait."

"I'm awfully sorry . . ."

"Just go ahead."

The briefcase close to his chest, the bureaucrat moved on back to the door that was painted the same as the wall, a deep silver that was almost gray. The door was easily overlooked, yet the bureaucrat picked his way as if knowing just where to go. Instructions were clear and concise, they didn't want fumbling or any questions. A short, patterned knock, the signal all customers used, then a deep existential sigh, the sort of sigh that one makes when life is too slow.

The door opened, admitting a sliver of light just enough for a person to pass. The bureaucrat drew a deep breath as if bracing himself for the room—the men waiting inside, the step that came next and would change everything forever—then he disappeared in the light. The door made the silver wall whole as if closing over a wound.

The room wasn't known or advertised to the people, and most seemed to follow a recommendation from someone who heard the rumors. Did the government help operations, keeping them on the sly? Not hardly, the pianist thought, not even here in Japan. The room existed in the ambiguity of a haiku poem, although it offered a concrete service that answered to genuine needs. The men came from all over Tokyo, in fact, all over the country, seeking ways of escape they could find nowhere else.

The pianist had never entered, and whoever was in the room ended work long after his shift. He imagined a sort of office, desks with folders and notes and the muted clacking of keyboards, men in suits asking questions in somber, uninvested voices, explaining logistics and steps and the fees, the how of the disappearance. To up and leave and be gone, the art of becoming air in the shape of a question mark.

The evaporated, they were called, the ones who were sealed and had started new lives somewhere else. Hundreds of people would vanish each year, fleeing circumstances such as debt or a family burden they couldn't bear, a list of misfortunes and shameful sins that had made their lives unendurable. The room passed no judgment and never asked questions, the same way that it promised no healing. In the language of business, however, you could say it provided solutions. There were cash advances, new names and locales and identities, a new family register if needed. Any measure to help ensure no one saw you leave or could understand what had happened. A trained staff, a small team of experts worked hard on erasing the past and leaving loose ends forever. A reinvention, a smooth letting go without trace.

When the last notes of the waltz had faded and the pianist wrapped the first set, the barman motioned him over. Dressed as he usually was in a uniform vest and bow tie, the barman was handsome with honest eyes, a thin mustache, and full moussed hair. The pianist approached on his guard since the two of them rarely talked, then he climbed up on the cushioned stool and there arranged himself with the sort of care one might expect from an older person. The barman poured out a drink, unprompted and on the house, then placed it before the pianist, who silently nodded his thanks. A highball, a large cube of ice, as smooth and pure as a dream.

"Not really slammed." The pianist sipped on the highball. It was cold and burned pleasantly in his throat.

"Too slow for me. Don't expect any more guests, not on a Sunday and with this rain."

The barman used English, as always with the pianist. He had the amiable manner of barmen all over the world, a man who follows most sports and remembers old times and friends.

"I like slow," the pianist said. "Trains ain't crowded, I can get a seat. Need to rest the old weary bones."

The barman was stroking his chin, as though giving the matter more thought. After years of working together, he realized he knew almost nothing about the pianist and his life before. The man was private, almost secretive about his personal affairs, and through his short and ambiguous answers about his family and friends, even hobbies, he had reached an extent of mysteriousness that precluded any further questions. One night, the barman had come in early and found the pianist alone by the window, looking out on the town below with what seemed to be tears in his eyes. He wasn't yet at the age where a foreigner ends up in a lounge, far away from the place of his birth.

"You have always played the piano?" the barman asked suddenly.

The pianist thought for a moment, slowly turning the glass on the coaster.

"Not always, not in another life. A line cook, then in the army, the last honest buck I made." He smiled at his own little joke, which hadn't registered with the barman.

"You were in the army?"

"Two tours of duty, discharged with honor. Ask anyone around. Shipped out for the East and ended up here, searching for bliss and the dharma Buddha."

"Army, *ne*? That is something."

The barman nodded without asking the questions on his mind. For a while they sat there in silence as the rain outside slowed, pattering against the window the way a taiko drum starts a number.

"There is something I wanted to ask you. A bit of advice, I suppose." The barman had mustered his courage. "Of course, you don't have to answer. The whole thing must seem rather strange."

"Let's hear it. Sunday night is the time for strange."

The barman nodded knowingly, then cleared his throat.

"I never mentioned I've been seeing this girl, you know, this American girl. An advisor with one of those firms, asset management in Marunouchi. One night she comes in for a drink—alone and a little shy, not talking too much. I could sense that she liked me, she just wasn't a typical American."

He glanced at the pianist, relieved there was no offense. "So, we go to have lunch, a place with Korean barbecue, and when we sit down and look at the menu and I ask is she ready to order, she looks up and says, 'Never mind.' Like, she isn't hungry. She'll have only water, no food at all. I was shocked, like, did I pick the wrong place? The wrong food or the atmosphere? I ask her what is the matter, is she on a diet or not feeling right? Would she like to go home? And she makes a strange smile and says, 'Nothing, not feeling like eating, just not really feeling hungry.' Then she sits there sipping the water and starts talking about her day, some problem she has at work. It was so strange, I couldn't order myself."

The barman looked sheepishly down at his hands. "A week later, we tried Chinese. The same thing—not feeling like eating. You understand this? A girl who keeps saying she isn't hungry? I've never dated an American before. It is normal, perhaps over there?"

For a moment they sat in silence, both lost in their personal thoughts. The barman checked for a refill, then unscrewed a bottle and topped off the highball, again on the house. His moves had a smooth and elegant grace, though he fussed less preparing a drink than most other barmen in Tokyo, a fact the pianist appreciated.

"My apologies," the barman said finally. "The whole thing is strange, never mind."

"How old is she? From where in the States?"

The pianist had the air of an expert, though in fact, he was at a loss. He had never met an American who sat down twice at a restaurant and then said she didn't want to eat. Was this a new generation of girls? And was her strangeness perhaps the reason why this particular girl had come to Japan?

"She is thirty or maybe older. She says she is from America, but in Japan, who can tell the difference? A foreigner can be anything and then Japanese people believe it. I wonder if she has a secret."

"A girl who says she ain't hungry . . ." The pianist swirled the vodka in his glass, weighing another sip. "It could mean she is actually hungry. Very hungry and needing to eat, just ain't showin, you know what I mean?"

The barman assumed this was the answer, as if somehow the matter was settled without offering any clue about the girl, when the piano man spoke again in a voice that suddenly trembled.

"Every corner there is damage, every goddamn corner. Everyone strange and full of themselves, everyone full of damage. You don't see it because they ain't showin, just ask anyone around."

He knocked back the drink in a punishing gulp, then lowered himself off the stool. On his way back to the piano, he turned around one more time, as though remembering another grievance.

"I ain't the expert, so why even ask me? I haven't been back there in years."

"My apologies, I didn't . . ."

Something about the hips, or maybe the legs. The way he swings out a foot, the awkward way he sits down. As if the legs are separate from the rest, as if somehow, he is getting used to them.

With an unhappy look on his face, thinking he hadn't much

helped with the problem facing the barman, the pianist returned to his instrument when a man from the group in the booth, the same guest who had made the request, sidled up to him once again. Amid copious nodding and bowing and apologies for the imposition, he requested the waltz one more time, "Thank you so much for changing it back—no, really, thank you so much."

They like what I do, the pianist mused, starting again on the waltz. But whether the chat with the barman had upset him or the highball diminished his grip, the new version came out as uneven, as shoddy in the bridge as before. The pedal messed up the legato, no more point for him in pretending this might be a matter of chords. He had only made it halfway through when the kabuki group rose to leave, engrossed in their conversation.

The pianist felt an unease that came partly from his mistakes, the damper he couldn't control. The notes knew where they had to go, only his grip wasn't able to follow. A matter of nerves and frustration, the old need to show he could play. As he fumbled through another bridge and sweat showed on his straining face, as if something essentially important depended on getting the waltz just right, his thoughts slipped away from his dancing fingers, first a little, then so far that no one could have guessed. He could see the old windswept mountain, an armored truck that had stalled and a shape aflame in the night, as life changed in a matter of moments and then for the rest of his days. From there, in a strange mental link, his thoughts returned to the locked silver door, the room in the back and the bureaucrat. Never mean, never making a scene, the men who came in to be sealed. They were calm—almost too calm, it seemed, an astounding show of restraint. It suddenly struck him as odd, not the attitude you would expect. No drama from the vamoosed, no shouting and tears or messy despair as lives were upended, reshuffled and strange, and fate was imposing a loss they would have to bear on their own. They could have ended things any time, there were platforms and trains all around, and yet they had chosen to come here.

The pianist looked out the window, the moonlight on empty avenues that were closed for traffic on weekends. The next corner was the old *depato*, the store with the large clock on top, now shuttered, unable to sell. Another hour and he could go home, perhaps have a seat on the train and rest the old weary bones.

The barroom sank into slumber, uneventfully numb with its peace. Time passed slowly and without any hurt as an empty shoe slipped on a damper, a phantom in over its head.

These people, the pianist mused, they sure like a way to escape.

Pelicans of Japantown

AS IF ON a cue, the birds lifted off and then rose, catching the ocean current in a smooth formation of four. A flapping of wings, so easy it was hardly visible, had them sailing off above the water that glistened like silvery hairnets. For a moment, they hung in the air, suspended, framed against the blue sky in the manner of an Ozu pillow shot. The image was striking, then gone, lost to the memory of the world.

A breeze teased the hair of the woman as she sat watching the foaming waves. Her clothes weren't for a beach—green pantsuit and heels—and the way she sat next to the man could make you assume they were strangers, when in fact, the man worked for the woman, and they had spent the last day together. Neither of them talked very much, not sure what to say that the other could understand.

On their way back from the house, a shuttered bungalow in the Sunset where a patrol cop had let them in, they had grabbed water and sandwiches at a market, then stopped at the beach to take in the sunset. Fuentes hadn't touched his sandwich, his stomach a shell without signal, but he watched with intrigue as the woman ate half of hers. With total focus, she unwrapped the pastrami, messy on a sourdough roll, then took the packets with mayo and mustard to add some more delicate sprinkles. The seasoning done, she put the packets back in the wrapping paper, arranged herself in a perfect posture, and then took a small, delicate bite. Her eyes closed, absorbed in the unknown taste.

Fuentes had never seen anyone eat a pastrami sandwich like that. A thing of appreciation, as if the sandwich was as important as anything the woman might do that day. He kept watching her for a while, oddly touched, until he needed to close his mind to the sandwich and the deep blue sky, the waves and the smell of the sea. The beauty held expectations, things that might overwhelm him.

"Are Japanese beaches like this? I mean, same ocean and all?"

Megumi looked up between bites. "In Chiba, we can enjoy with surfing. The sea is more dark, not like here. Anyway, I'm from Tokyo."

"No beaches there?"

"Excuse me?"

"I mean, no beaches in Tokyo?"

"Not beaches, no. We work hard, then rest on the weekend."

Megumi smiled an uncertain smile, revealing some crooked teeth. Fuentes wished he could speak her language, a language that for him existed only in movies where nobody surfed. He had more questions about Tokyo and beaches, he just wasn't sure how to talk to this woman. He liked driving her around town, the way she had brought a purpose to his previously unstructured days. Only sometimes, she left him confused. The way she fussed over each receipt no matter how small the amount, or how she kept shading her small, slender face in order to keep it from tanning. The weather was her obsession and she kept asking him what she should wear, the number of layers to dress for the forecast, which in this place, he kept telling her, wasn't possible.

Megumi gave up on questions, afraid that she might look stupid. The man knew the town and the locals, but she frowned on his strange appearance, the hollow cheeks and the long blonde hair. A bald patch on top, the sides falling loose onto narrow shoulders, the look made her think of the *ochimusha* from the time of the civil wars. If a samurai fled from battle, away from the master he had failed and without the courage for ritual suicide, he had to signal his shame to the world by untying his hair from the knot, leaving the sides to hang from a top that was shaved. The ochimusha were the dishonored, a style no man in Japan would choose.

The mission was so confidential, so embarrassing for the authorities back in Japan, that it called for a local liaison who could keep things under his hat. Megumi had in fact wondered where the consulate found her man. He was kind and generous with his time and during breaks in her schedule had shown her the sights, the famous red bridge, and the park with the Japanese garden. It was just that he seemed preoccupied, as if a shadow were on his mind. She didn't know that Fuentes was absent because his stomach made painful twitches, that he wished he hadn't stopped for the view and was thinking with the foresight of an addict—a man carefully measuring time and distances in terms of his imminent needs— how long it was back to the hotel and then across town to meet his connect, a *traficante* down in the Mission.

"We must find Oshiro," Megumi said earnestly. "The consulate is very concerned." She drew in her feet, though the waves weren't lapping close. "I hope the club has more information."

Fuentes had started shaking, holding his upper arms. Even more than the awful sickness, the nausea and the aches that haunted every waking moment, he feared that the woman might notice that something was wrong with her driver. As she was wrapping the rest of her sandwich and a wave foamed a line on the sand, the ocean he used to love with its endless slowness of days, he scratched his arm trying to remember if the toaster was already pawned.

Out at sea, the sun glistened on an ocean freighter moving slowly on the horizon. The pelicans were long gone, off to the place where pelicans go when the sun falls into the sea.

Alone back in her hotel room, a suite that overlooked Union Square, Megumi enjoyed a long shower that steamed up the marble bath, then chose her clothes for the next day. She had brought four pairs of socks and underwear, one for each day, and now one remained in her suitcase. The others were in the garbage, not a hamper for dirty laundry. She had purposely packed old clothes she could throw away after wear, leaving space in her case for souvenirs. An old travel hack among Japanese people, it was her way of tackling the mission, her first time alone in America.

A new man in the passport section, Oshiro had vanished somewhere in Las Vegas, along with an attaché case that was filled with Japanese passports. An email from the Bellagio, an hour after checking in, then he had dropped off the face of the earth. Without a trace, almost two hundred Japanese passports, newly minted and needed for imminent travel, had vanished with the man who carried them. A riddle inside an enigma, a screwup of epic proportions.

Once a year in the summer months, a staff from the Japanese consulate flew from San Francisco out to Las Vegas, to arrange for new passports in the area. They would stay for a couple of days, collecting the expired documents from Japanese tour guides and chefs and dancers, then come back the next month with new issues. As a rule, a tidy procedure—but not with Oshiro. He never showed up for the delivery, leaving residents without passports as trips overseas were on hold. Amid mounting hassles and inconveniences, the consulate was barraged with complaints, expat workers asking with irritation what sort of customer service was this?

Megumi had no great hopes for the results of her fact-finding mission. She resisted at first when the chief at the Foreign Ministry had asked her to look into the matter, thinking it dangerous to go to America and investigate what might be a crime. Strange things happened here, she knew from the movies and personal stories. She had dated an American once, years back in a reckless summer, and the breakup had torn out her heart and smashed it into little pieces.

As she turned on the massive television and then switched from channel to channel, flicking past news and the constant commercials and then settling on what seemed like a comedy, she wasn't able to understand anything. She had looked forward to American television, but the rapid, excited language seemed transmitted from another planet, where aliens spoke and behaved in ways that to her were incomprehensible.

The phone rang. It was Fuentes.

"I'm sorry . . . I know it's late. Everything still all right? The room is okay?"

He hadn't asked before, his voice now warm with concern. A stash of the rest was safe in his pocket.

"I was just going to sleep." Megumi muted the TV. "The room is nice, especially the shower. Much larger than Japanese showers."

"Remember, you shouldn't go out after dark. Too sketchy, even around the hotel. One block safe, the next one ain't. Never one when things get weird."

He paused, having said his piece and not wanting to say goodbye. "Get some rest," he said finally. "Tomorrow is your last day."

"You've been very kind. Tomorrow after the club, perhaps you are busy? I was thinking to eat in Japantown."

"I'm meeting some friends, not sure we . . ." His voice drifted off. "The room is good, the phone works? You call the folks in Japan?"

"I'm sorry?"

"Your family . . ."

"We just talked. Everybody is doing fine." She hadn't touched the phone on the desk, unsure how to dial and whom she should call.

"Always good to connect with family," said Fuentes. He hadn't heard from his own in years and tried hard not to think of his mother, who said contact was out of the question until he faced what she called "the bad business," or at least made a little gesture by getting her mink out of hock. Fuentes was quick to admit that things were entirely his fault; he just wasn't able to change. He once had a friend, a fellow addict who liked to say, "It ain't me, it's the habit." Fuentes liked the idea, the sense that the habit did things of its own that his better side just couldn't stop. But when he had tried the line with his family, no one believed what he said.

Megumi hung up, then went over to the window and looked down on the square full of tourists. She was pondering the word "sketchy," the term that Fuentes had used. A drawing sketch, or like comedy? It didn't make any sense to her.

A cable car clanged, the bell syncopating the night as she emerged on the street. A siren wailed past and a man in a wheelchair, teeth amiss and no time, muttered angrily under his breath as he pushed the wobbly contraption. A group of women strode with a swagger, dressed for a night on the town and talking with absolute confidence, the voices, the laughter of the television. A surge of life filled Megumi, moving her down the streets so unlike the order of Tokyo. The crowd was pumped for the night, the air filled with a sense of adventure, with dangers she couldn't name. She hadn't traveled much in her life and seldom went out back home, not even after the breakup had freed up much of her time.

Charmed by the foreignness that surrounded her, the palm trees that touched the night sky, the sidewalks sparkling like fairy dust, she reached Market Street and went down to Van Ness, then cut back through a row of blocks that the locals considered sketchy. Alarmed by the change in the streets, the underside of the town she now crossed, she hastened through squalor and smells that were mean in the dark, passing stores with sprayed shuttered fronts and shapes slumped in tenement doorways, then a building where, hours before, the police had arrested two men and netted a cache of narcotics.

The hallways were hush with midnight, her room dark as she returned. Another shower, a touch of cold cream, then the queen bed engulfed her shape. As she sank into sleep, exhausted, her last thoughts returned to home and a life that seemed suddenly small. She never wondered if she was lonely or if things were missing from her life. She felt these were dangerous thoughts. But alone now in her hotel room, far away from her Tokyo routines, she would not only allow the questions, but her answers were shockingly clear. The streets were shaking from engines as she moved through surrealist dreams, a series of strange adventures in shadowy urban nights. For the first time in a long while, she wasn't grinding her teeth in her sleep.

In a rooming house in the Mission that doubled as a shooting gallery, above the gate of a storefront church and a taqueria known for its pork enchiladas, Fuentes sat on an unmade bed. He was calm now, swaying in his underwear. On his forehead was a pale sweat that mirrored the sheen of a lamp, the sole source of light in the room. The air held a note of vinegar that came from a pouch on the sheets, imported from south of the border and sold on the street by a man with no teeth. Not commonly used in Mexican food, it was an ominous smell in these parts.

He felt for the lamp on the nightstand next to the small wooden cross, the photo of three marines tucked into the frame of a mirror. Finding the switch, he ended the dimness. Night had arrived and would bring the great rest, to swallow him up until dawn. A summons of helpless dopamine, transforming the walls into oceans.

A norteño polka wafted in from outside, the kitchen had started the dishes. An accordion full of life, a tuba getting ahead of itself. The music was calming to Fuentes, the background of his nightly ritual. The connect had discounted the stash as part of a weekend special, other rooms now held similar rests. An optometrist from El Centro muttered in a dream without image.

Fuentes leaned back on the sheets, his eyes shut in anticipation. He waited for darkness to find him, the moment it took for the warmth to appease the nerve, then journey on subcutaneously and ease all the pain into numbness. He stopped all thinking and focused instead on his breath, one shallow inhale at a time. Again, he could be a baby, all need and no taxes. Selfishly hapless, asleep on a breast without end.

The warmth had made his life simple, had reduced all effort and expectation to a devotion that burned with purpose. The one thing he needed to have, the reason he had always needed to renounce the ways of the world. Nothing to chase beyond the next stash, nothing to prove to himself or anyone besides scraping up funds for the rest. He loved how the drugs allowed him to travel, allowed him to see and experience what was otherwise out of reach.

As night inched along and the accordion began to fade, Fuentes could sense the warmth as it moved along through his veins, carrying blood and shame to the heart. He knew that a part of him wanted to die, that he had no tools to deny the warmth the thing it would ask in the end.

The sun was setting behind the slope on which stood the mall of Japantown, casting shadows on the peace pagoda, the plaza where they were sitting. Women with shopping bags came out of stores, while dinner parties and families sat down at the sushi restaurants. Megumi had tried a rice ball with eel from a shop, then realized sadly that it had no taste.

"We are early. They open at nine."

Fuentes looked more disheveled in blue denim jeans and a tasseled vest, a stubble on his oval face, yet inside, he was filled with calm. He had slept until late afternoon and was comfortably numb from the rest, a stash for the night in his pocket.

"You are sure this is the right place?"

"It's Japantown. All Japanese people come here."

Megumi made no response, not sure what he meant. No Japanese roamed the place that was mostly a couple of malls full of families who looked like tourists. Besides a small branch of Daiso, nothing resembled modern Japan.

"Are you from San Francisco? I mean, born here?"

"South Bend, Indiana. Came after the army, then stayed for the weather. The people, the scene—it was great."

Fuentes looked at Megumi, surprised to see she was listening. Funny, he mused, he hadn't thought of these things in years.

"I worked at a shop, fixing cars. Most summers I traveled or hung with friends for a while. A guy in Bolinas, his mom down there owned a house. Two minutes and you were surfing or fishing at one of the piers. Nothing to do but look at the ocean, shooting the breeze with the boys. Back then, this place wasn't just for rich people. No one cared how much dough you had."

His side hair danced in the wind, exposing his neck, the tattoo he had there. A faded eagle, artfully inked, above the words "divided we fall."

Megumi mused about her companion. She thought suddenly that he looked manly, a man in his own domain living by rules he had made for himself. Unlike her image of strong Americans who were always on top of the world, he seemed to be holding a sadness, as though he lost something very important and didn't know how to get it back. She liked his patience and humble attitude, how he waited for her despite his other commitments. She wondered about his age and if he was ever married.

"What is next for you? More work for the consulate?"

Fuentes looked down at his hands. "You know, stuff comes up . . . but there's this shop in the Mission, down on Dolores. Trucking solutions. Looks like business is picking up."

"That sounds nice. Americans work hard, like Japanese."

Megumi couldn't picture the shop or what trucking solutions might look like, but the fact was, neither could Fuentes. His room had two nights on the rent and there was no more deposit left, so he expected to get the boot and find himself on the street. Having realized he could keep his money if he simply stopped paying his bills, he planned to move into the Fiesta and park near a school overnight, resigned to whatever was next on the spiral he couldn't stop.

"I once dated an American. In Tokyo, some years ago."

Megumi was shocked to hear herself say this. She had responded to Fuentes' openness, the intimacy among strangers. Now that the mission was almost completed and she was about to return to Japan, she didn't think they would meet again.

"It was nice at first," she went on. "But then later, it was so difficult. Always fighting and making up, I never knew why."

"What was it about? The fighting, I mean."

Megumi thought for several moments, as if for the very first time. "I was lonely," she said at last.

The sun and the shoppers were gone, a chill reaching the bench where they sat. "Perhaps try the club now?" Megumi straightened her pantsuit.

The search of the house by the ocean, messy and slightly depressing in the way of a young man abroad, had reaped a clue in the shape of a business card. Megumi had called the Pink Blossom, a hostess club in Japantown, where after a few innocuous questions, the *mama-san* recalled Oshiro and shared some more information.

"He came to the club on weekends, usually when he was bored. But I haven't seen him for weeks."

"He went to Las Vegas for work." Megumi was speaking faster, excited there was a trail. "You have spoken to him after that?"

"One night, yes. Very late. We were just closing." The mama-san's voice became wary. "You said you are with the consulate?"

"A liaison from Tokyo. Did he—"

"This isn't something I'd discuss on the phone. Feel free to stop by at the club. I'm here most nights after nine."

The Pink Blossom wasn't easy to find, a door unmarked in the depth of a mall. By the time they stood at the entrance in a dim corner of the Japan Center, most of the corridors lay abandoned, the restaurants closed for the night. The hostess answering the chime seemed to wonder what was more perplexing, a Japanese woman with crooked teeth, or a sketchy-looking American with the hair of a spineless samurai.

"By appointment?" she asked, leaving the chain on the door.

The place was a transport, a throwback from the 1970s to a fantasy of Japan in the '50s, which, in fact, made it not unlike a hostess club in modern Tokyo. Seated in back and waiting for the proprietress, Fuentes was stunned by the setup. He had passed Japantown a million times delivering pizza or catching some jazz at the Fillmore without knowing the club existed. It was bigger inside than he had imagined from outside. On a small karaoke stage, an old man was serenading the room along with computer drums and a shamisen, while off to the sides in the dim velvet booths sat men talking to women who laughed at all of their jokes. Time surely had overlooked this place.

"A kind man, hadn't been here for long." Minae had joined them, a mama-san in her sixties who sat facing them in the booth.

"Oshiro asked for me, never one of the girls. He came in late and sat at the bar, quiet and by himself. Always ordered Santori, same as back home."

In a kimono and the thick makeup of middle age, Minae used English for Fuentes' sake. The strange look of the American man made her think of a gruesome movie she had seen as a little child, where a dishonored samurai was slain and his severed head displayed on a pole, the side hair limp in the rain. Minae shivered remembering the image.

"The consulate has been worried," said Megumi. "We haven't heard from Oshiro-san."

"The work was hard, he often complained. The rules and responsibility, and him just fresh out of college."

As if seeing things in a flashback, Minae shut her eyes under brows that were plucked to delicate arches. "Some of the passports he handled were old, some even smelled. Some Japanese hide their passports, stuffed in a shoe on the plane."

"Passports in shoes?" Megumi was stunned, checking Fuentes

to see if he followed.

"They naturalize, become Americans. But some of them keep their passports, even though they are not supposed to. Japanese can't be dual citizens."

Fuentes nodded, eyes absent. He wasn't able to follow the talk, but he had just about figured things out. He knew that the passports were lost and that Minae was covering for Oshiro. A night on the strip and a man cutting loose, the neon and games, a bureaucrat thinking there must be a system. A winning streak, then the losing, one more round, just one more round, throwing good money after bad and then desperate after good until the last, devastating cleanout. A briefcase left at a table, then snatched by a stranger, because Japanese people are targets. Or maybe a briefcase snatched by a hooker, Oshiro-san gone on cocaine in a suite up at the Bellagio. A shocking of raw temptation among lemons in trembling slots, the fountains that danced to the music, then shame the next day and a hasty departure. It happens to a man on the road, no judgment here from Fuentes. He knew the odds of beating the house and getting away with the feat, and he respected a man who had slipped. A man with hard thoughts about honor, swaying alone in arcane hotels.

Minae cleared her throat softly. "Oshiro-san always hated when the consulate took their passports, when Japanese lost their citizenship. Like stealing their shadow, he said. He hated that part of the job."

She looked at Megumi. "Can you believe it? Needing a visa to go to Japan? Like there is no home, no more country."

"We didn't hear from him after Las Vegas. Did he tell you about the trip?"

"He seemed changed, almost shocked." Minae waved over a hostess and murmured some serving instructions before turning again to Megumi and resuming in quick Japanese. After a while, remembering Fuentes, she switched back to fluent English.

"I cannot tell you what happened exactly. It would cause great shame for Oshiro-san." Minae lowered her eyes, then rose from the table. "It is shameful but cannot be helped. My sincerest apologies."

"Minae-san..."

"Please don't look for him. He isn't here and you cannot find him. Please accept his humble apologies."

"Is he all right?" Megumi was anxious.

Minae considered her answer, her face lined from the secrets of men who had traveled through nights on seas of cheap sake. After what seemed like a very long time, she shook her head slowly, almost imperceptibly, then her eyes lowered, end of discussion.

Just like that. Not all right.

Another old man on the clubroom stage was belting out karaoke, a homesickness blues from Hiroshima echoing along the walls. The words struck Fuentes with a sense of romantic loss, evoking exile and things of the past. As the pain came back to his stomach in a way that made him fear the worst, he felt a pang of enormous regret and then knew what the song was about. A stroll in the sun, the light in the morning trees. The autumnal Ashida River, a moment that couldn't come back.

The search ended there, inconclusive. Whatever happened in Vegas or somewhere else, Oshiro-san and the passports weren't likely ever to be found. A staircase into the ocean, a ghost in the sunset as birds watched above, bewildered.

Megumi thought that it couldn't be helped, convinced that her findings, once summed up in a report, should meet with official approval. They would think about what had happened and conduct more education for employees, then send new passports with bows of contrition and promises to do better. Having wrapped up the mission and said goodbye to the consulate staff, Megumi was down to her final underwear and readying for departure. She had wondered about the evening, her last night in San Francisco, the farewell to her loyal driver. He looked sad coming out on the plaza as they walked over to the Ford, and on a whim, she had asked to join him as he moved along to his party. Immediately, his face lit up. She would dig it, he kept assuring, they all would just love to meet her. Megumi wondered about the digging and how this was part of a party.

The house was out in the avenues, near the zoo at the end of the town where the monkeys perched in the mist. A seagull cried overhead, the air smelling like dunes and the sea that peeked dimly at the horizon. The streets were shrouded in white, making it hard for Fuentes to see and he almost went past the place. An adobe with yellow windows, the driveway blocked with aged cars. An ancient Impala dented and shamed, a lowered Camaro with plastic-bag windows that flapped like the sails of distress.

"No worries, it don't mean nothing. Some new people, another flavor." Fuentes leaned on the doorbell, evoking a chime.

"Your coworkers?"

"Something like that. There's much more to see in this town."

"I can visit now that I know someone here." Megumi smiled and Fuentes smiled back, suppressing a twitch in his stomach.

The disorientation was instant, an immersion of sights and sound, yet the thing that most struck Megumi was the smell assailing her nose. Unable to place the aroma—the scent that seeped thickly through the rooms without seeming to have a source—she had wanted to ask Fuentes but lost him the moment they entered. Her eyes scanned the cluttered kitchen, a dish made of rice and meats like nothing she knew from Japan. She couldn't join any of the conversations, hearing languages that weren't English and accents of incomprehension that seemed to make talk impossible. She thought this place could not be America, then she realized she didn't know what America was like. Amid salvos of alien merriment that rippled the hallway crowds, she felt like she was underwater and watched fish move their tiny mouths, then disperse and move to new groups.

From the living room came a salsa, percussive and smooth. The furniture was moved to the wall, the dance floor all faces and bodies as men were light on their feet to the flow of the sensuous beat. Megumi looked round in shock. No women were in the house—just her, alone with these men, none of whom she had ever met. She almost gasped, then she realized none of the dancers were paying her any mind. No eyes, not even a glance as couples in white shirts and denim moved under the spell of the music, synchronized in their steps and dreaming in unison. A couple swayed past with hairless heads shimmering, their goatees so impeccably clipped that a match would light on their cheeks.

"You know Fuentes? Have you seen him?"

The men shook their heads almost mournfully.

As she was starting to enjoy the dance, her feet picking up the beat as a man took her by the hand and led—one step forward, two to the side—the hallway upstairs was eerily quiet. Fuentes was in a room, alone, slumped on a davenport sofa under a poster of Cher in the '70s. The phone in his vest rang eagerly, almost panicked, as he trembled in spasms that left him no breath. Suddenly, he became still, his frame slipping off the davenport. Just like that: not all right. Alone in a room with shortening breath, a tube dropped from his clammy hand into the folds of a shaggy rug. A foghorn moaned from the bay, a ship calling out in the night.

As Fuentes sank into rest, the mother of all rest forever, a helpless part of his mind searched for snippets of explanation. The pain hitting hard and his head on fire, he had gone upstairs to lie down. The first time, he tried the inhale from the batch of the new connect—maybe laced with some animal tranquilizer or a manner of inexact science from our friends down south of the border—because fools will buy at a discount and then that is how some fools die. A pelican catching a current, then fading away in the dusk.

Time slowed, then stopped altogether. Through the warmth and a haunting remorse, Fuentes could see the ocean—the waves and the endless sky, a woman preparing a beautiful sandwich—and he could see these things as new rituals, could allow them to be near and dear. Their names were beginnings at last, untouched by the awful waste.

"Fuentes . . . what's happened?"

A look had her by the sofa—eyes wide, afraid. In the ancient manner of women tending to men who have fallen in war, she first held, then unbent the shape to open the denim jacket. A stranger out of her depths whom he met only days before, a stranger left in his charge to be safe in a foreign place. He liked her, liked her so much, for she was the path to new names, a promise he mustn't lose. A small woman with crooked teeth and the arms of a little girl, the last piece of earthly reality as darkness came closing in. It took awful strength, then the words came.

"Will you marry me? At the beach?"

A strain muttered feebly, then time hung empty between them. His lips seemed to move and draw breath, as Megumi brushed a strain from his face. She ached to keep him from leaving as she looked into his small warm eyes, caressing his hollow cheeks.

"Of course," she whispered. "Of course, I will marry you."

The Rain in Nagoya

SACHIKO LIKED WHEN it rained on Fridays. It was something most people found strange, but in Japanese, she could have explained.

The rain made her want to go out and explore the place where she lived. There were obstacles, of course, the wind turning your umbrella and throwing the cold in your face, the elements making it harder to go and enjoy the weekend. You had to weigh the rewards, then check your resolve and decide. How much did you really want to have fun? Was the excitement worth getting wet?

The rain came down the windows like aquarian music as Sachiko descended from the loft. Up in the bed was a man she had been seeing for almost three weeks, an investment for him whose return she had promised, then withheld as a tease, then granted at last on this night. She wouldn't see the man ever again, wouldn't call him again or act like she was interested in his work or the folk songs he wrote on the guitar.

Sachiko slipped down the ladder and onto the floor, her heart beating a little faster. Searching the floor and the furniture in the dark, her clothes scattered in a random map, she picked up her bra, the tank top, and the lavender pleated skirt, then dressed herself without sound. On a teak cabinet in the hallway, she left a small, handwritten note.

This is it—please don't call.

The man might call anyway, she expected, leaving increasingly urgent messages as the days wore on and the silence piled up. He didn't know where she lived, no connection could help him find her. Time would pass until eventually he read the clues and interpreted the silence as curtains, a plea to move on without scenes. Perhaps he would see her as evil and curse the day they had met, or perhaps he would shrug and forget her and eventually meet somebody new. Either way, Sachiko wished the man well.

Tiptoeing on the hardwood floor, she crossed the hallway and then the living room, ignoring the view of the bay. She reached the door and slipped into her sandals, then let herself out of the house and into the freedom of the night.

Once in her Mazda parked awkwardly on a hill, Sachiko turned on the music, then leaned back in the seat with eyes closed. A while later, she took a chocolate egg from her purse, peeled off the wrapper and began munching with absent bites. As her tongue ran over her teeth and the sticky-sweet caramel in her mouth, her mind was on Nine Inch Nails, the orchestra of meaning erased. Alone in the car with the pain of Trent Reznor massaging the speakers, Sachiko felt comfortable and safe, as if carried to a faraway place where no one and nothing could reach her. The sound was a barrier to the darkness, the things she could not understand.

Pulling away from the house and then drifting downhill toward Market, the moonless streets so much darker than residential streets in Japan, she made her way home under clouds and fog that seemed to be holding more rain.

All in all, she thought, the first time had been a success.

Once a month on her day off, Sachiko volunteered as an educator. She visited high schools in the Bay Area and helped with workshops about condoms and saying no, about boundaries and choices and the parameters of sexual abuse. Using discussions and role play, she taught the students that they owned their bodies, that no one should touch them if it didn't feel right, and that they should never be pressured to keep a secret, not even by a family member. It was important, fulfilling work—on the website of her organization a girl commented, "I feel stronger and safe," and Sachiko knew she was at her best when she was teaching, giving all she had to the class. She enjoyed interacting with children, enjoyed their intuitive questions that checked if adults were safe. They looked her straight in the eyes and believed what they saw there.

The work was one reason why she liked America. At home in Nagoya, where the trains reserved cars for women to be safe from the groping of *chikan*, it was rare for teachers in school to view sex from a female perspective. Sachiko liked that America was different. Much as she missed onsen baths and relaxing soaks, much as she longed to rejoin her old friends for afternoon tea or a night out at karaoke, her work and her freedom were more important. She was stunned by how American women could change partners without social disapproval, sleeping with men like men slept with women. If Sachiko could do the same, reeling men in like enamored fish and discarding them at a time of her choosing, it might mean she was like an American.

Getting noticed was never difficult. The city was a giant meat market for youth who were working in tech, a moneyed international scene open to exploration. Many men, and frequently women, were curious about a Japanese date, professing interest in Asian culture as they searched online for a roommate or a partner for language exchange. Many years after Hiroshima and Nagasaki had been haunted by *pika don*, the flash and boom melting humans like tragic wax into pavement, Japan was a brand in America, the sashimi and salmon served on clay plates in expensive restaurants.

Sachiko was struck by the difference between American men and Japanese. Americans were taller and louder and would take over conversations, which made talking to them almost similar to watching a show on TV. The moment some men would start with a lengthy explanation, she tuned out and just watched the show without any need to contribute, occasionally checking to see if their lips were still moving. On the plus side, they were sweet and attentive and even held doors to let women go first, a sign of respect that Sachiko found amazing.

Since arriving a few months back, she had met other Japanese women who had made new lives in America. They were interesting—active and strong, full of life. One of them was Tomomi, a smart, sassy girl from an affluent family in Osaka. The way they had bonded was surprising, but then, overseas we have different friends.

An occasional model with some blonde in her short-clipped hair, Tomomi was seeing a lawyer from Pasadena, a man in his forties whose younger brother was also dating a Japanese woman.

One night over margaritas, Tomomi explained the rules of attraction and how Americans saw women like them. Sachiko was surprised to see her stock raised, but then it made sense. American men were looking for a break, exhausted by their own women and the endless fight for equality. They were on the ropes, Tomomi explained, the hot breath of pursuit in their back as they sensed the fair sex closing in, women working harder and harder to have everything that the men had. With Japanese women, the distance seemed safer, the challenges less direct. Or at least that was the idea.

"A Western man dreaming of geisha," Tomomi affected a bow, "is gonna do whatever you want."

"You mean that I have a free choice?"

"More choice than you'll know what to do with."

Sachiko liked Tomomi, her independence and easy spirit. Only sometimes, she couldn't understand her. So different from women back home, as if she were lost in between the worlds and thinking she was American. So loud and full of opinions that Japanese people would think her troublesome.

She can't go back, Sachiko mused with mild disapproval. They will think she is someone from space.

The night after climbing down from the loft, Sachiko dreamed she was in Japan. She often had dreams of Japan where she met family and friends or enjoyed some Japanese food, but this particular one struck her as strange.

On a train headed for Nagoya, dressed in a dark business suit, slacks, and sneakers, she was hurrying from one car to the next, weaving through crowds of anonymous businessmen as she looked for the women's compartment. The train was enveloped by rain and Sachiko kept checking her watch with a growing sense of unease, afraid she was late for a meeting. After what seemed like a very long time, she reached a narrow, elongated tube, where a sign on a bulging door read, "For safe and strong women only." The car was empty save for a girl who was perched on the edge of her seat, a short redhead of eleven or twelve, wearing a skirt and a yellow top with a print that said "D IS FOR DOG."

"Hello there," Sachiko said.

"Hello." The girl dangled her feet from the seat.

"You look familiar. Have we met before?"

The girl looked up, curious. She had large round eyes, like comforting pools. Her heels tapped softly against the front of the seat: one, two.

"Your talk the other day, it was nice." Her voice was matter-of-fact.

"Thank you, I tried my best. I was actually a bit nervous."

"We should learn things like that, you know. Because everyone has a body."

Sachiko nodded, struck by the hair of the girl that shone in the light of the seat.

Waking up, she felt strangely confused, almost sad in a way she couldn't explain. Too bad there hadn't been time to respond to the little girl. She had wanted to explain things more because the girl was right, it was important, and everyone had a body.

Sachiko hardly experienced the act in terms of her own needs and pleasure. She wasn't wild or generous in bed, and the man she had left on the loft had voiced subtle disappointment. A lover in Japan called her *maguro*—a tuna fish with eyes closed, her arms hanging slack to the side. Sachiko thought that this couldn't be helped, couldn't see why a man should care or why she owed him some sort of performance.

She liked to observe and take notes in her mind, a scholar of gender studies. She would follow the hastening breath and the skin aching for release, then the spasm that tightened features with a solemnness that seemed comical. Men needed women to be there, needed women to make it real—but then in the end, they were inward, a calmness behind their eyes that women no longer shared. The faces were interesting to Sachiko, as well as the shift of control before them. In the moments before the release, a mere flicker in time, yet so fiercely, eternally desired, so minutely arranged and earned with investment and earnest effort, it was the woman who held the power.

The night in the loft, when the man had turned over, exhausted, she lay still in her half of the bed. She was pleased and now waited to leave, and she hadn't expected the sorrow that suddenly fell over her heart. Aware of the need to talk before the man fell asleep and disappeared from her life forever, she asked a question she had prepared, a line from an American movie. Americans, she knew from Tomomi, often said things they had heard in movies as if their lives were a movie as well, a movie where they played the Americans.

"What magnitude was the earthquake?"

"Off the charts," the man muttered in the dark.

A new Friday night, the end of her new attachment. Seven-thirty and clouds kept amassing. The forecast predicted rain.

The city was beautiful in the sun, but the rain deprived it of charm and colors paled in an instant. The streets turned gray as the sky and the homeless were miserable, some riding the trains for hours, silent in medieval squalor, others shuffling along the sidewalk and mumbling obscurantist psalms, explaining, always explaining, describing themselves to the world with wet blankets trailing behind, indifferent to the mad buses that splashed up the flooding gutters. The cafés were empty and even the pastels looked glum, devoid of Victorian cheek.

Her hands on the wheel, Sachiko sat with eyes closed in the car, immersed in the teachings of Nine Inch Nails. She wore a mauve low-cut dress she had bought in Shibuya, a red wide-brimmed hat and open-toed sandals. In a pocket of her dress was the note.

She was parked on Union in the Marina, a street devoted to boutiques and nail salons and dogs that looked very expensive. Across from her was the restaurant, a new place for fusion cuisine that was booked for weeks in advance. Sachiko loved eating and trying new restaurants, and the food was part of her excitement. The man would treat her to a candlelight dinner, then to a bar for another drink and from there on to his place to close. "Americans close on the second date," Tomomi had said. "After that, it is wasting time."

Weeks after Easter, there was still chocolate in Sachiko's purse, an assortment of little eggs that were hiding in nooks and crannies. She had meant to cut down and eat only one egg per day, but the regimen was hard to maintain. Her mother complained on her last time home that Sachiko was gaining weight, that she looked frumpy and Americanized and would never find a husband in Japan, because all reasonable men there would pass on a cow fattened in the West. Her parents were very traditional and had already chosen her spouse, a salaryman at Toyota who lived down the street with a cat that they liked. Sachiko would rather stay exiled forever than marry a man of her father's choice. He was the last person to know what was right for her.

She took a chocolate egg from her purse and unwrapped it, then smoothed the wrapper and checked the calories. American chocolate had more sugar than Japanese, but also Americans were less strict about weight. Mindful of her mom's disapproval, she put the chocolate in her mouth, savoring the sweet taste. If her mother had any inkling of the trespass she planned for a little later on, the offense of a few extra pounds would have paled into insignificance.

The man came around a corner. Early thirties and handsome, shaved head and fashionable glasses, almost mythically Black in the way that he talked and moved. She had met him at a party, where Tomomi had introduced them. Conversation came easy, the attraction so tense between them it almost created static. He was in computers or finance or maybe financing of computers, she couldn't remember which. Initially, she had some concerns, unsure if she should use the term "Black" or should instead say "African-American." She had many such questions but was nervous to ask the man, afraid that she might sound ignorant, or worse, offend him as a person. She had scored going out with a Black man in America, both in terms of his looks and the shock he represented in Japan, and she was anxious for the date to go smoothly.

Sachiko watched the man enter the restaurant, then turned off the music and checked her makeup. About to head out, she faltered, sinking back into the seat. She looked herself over again, turning her cheeks in the rearview mirror and flicking a curl behind her left ear. Then she got out of the car and crossed to the restaurant.

"Hello, princess." The man rose as Sachiko came to the table, beating the hostess to offer a chair.

"Hello, my prince."

Sachiko quickly scanned his clothes and face, the way his shaved head shimmered in the candlelight. They had been dating for almost two weeks, going to bars in the Mission and making out in front of his apartment, which, to her surprise, he shared with a roommate to afford the expensive rent. From the way he was dressed now and carried himself with a coiled sort of confidence, Sachiko knew that tonight was the night, the time for her dream to come true.

"My favorite place in the city." The man smiled, showing perfect teeth. "I think you'll love it. They also have sushi, California rolls."

"Sounds nice."

Sachiko ran a hand through her hair, putting a spin on her voice. The man looked suddenly struck, an amorous deer in the headlights. It was an effect she still found amusing. The cognition of the neocortex was abandoned, the lizard brain taking over as thinking reduced to a primeval focus. From this moment on, Sachiko would be a body conversing with a penis.

"You look stunning," murmured the penis.

"You look nice, too."

Sachiko smiled, and the penis smiled back.

The waiter appeared with the leather-bound menus. A single page, three choices, no prices shown. The dishes were described with long lists of adjectives, many of them in French, and Sachiko struggled to make a decision while she was telling the man about Nagoya.

"We have an old castle, a golden fish on the top. And beautiful trees with cherry blossoms. In the spring, we have picnics under the trees, sitting down on blankets with food."

"Sounds nice." His eyes were fixed on the menu.

"I just talked to my friend, a girl in Nagoya. We've known each other since college and she is excited that we are dating. You know, because you are Black."

The man made a short, polite laugh, then amusement drained from his face. He grew thoughtful and then as he looked at her, his calm, confident voice held a note of vexation. "I hope you're not here just because I am Black. Not sure I'd be comfortable with that."

An awkward pause, as if playing cats had broken their toy.

Sachiko buried her face in the menu.

What was the problem? Why were her friends not supposed to be excited? And why had the man grown cold when her remark was meant as a compliment?

Without knowing the exact offense, there was no way for

Sachiko to apologize. Nothing like this had happened when she dated the man in the loft, but now she felt like entering a world full of complex, hidden entanglement. She had no concept, she realized, of who the man in front of her was—how clever he was, how shallow or sensitive. She almost panicked over the tension that had suddenly chilled the table, the sense that the date had derailed. She kept her eyes on the fancy menu without registering any of the text. In her pocket, the note burned a hole in her dress. *This is it—please don't call.*

With each second that passed, the gap in the banter became too long to be easily dismissed. Other dates might have liked her silence, viewing Sachiko as quietly mysterious, but the man appeared to hold back as if waiting for an explanation. Feeling confused, then ashamed of herself like a foreigner fresh off the boat, Sachiko started to resent the man for causing her this discomfort. She rose with a mumbled excuse and moved back along the plush carpet, sensing the eyes in her back.

Instead of turning to the bathrooms she went on past the velvety curtains, leaving the restaurant without claiming her hat, then crossed the street and got into the Mazda. She sat hunched in the seat for a while, listening to Nine Inch Nails and checking the rearview mirror. It was soothing to be alone with Trent Reznor, his anguished madness, and the longer she sat there and listened, the more she could see how the evening had derailed.

She wasn't feeling like California cuisine, not at all.

Sampling the dishes now in her mind, the smells and ingredients and textures, the way each bite would feel in her mouth, she concluded it was not what she wanted. What she wanted was a pork cutlet served with a miso-based sauce, a specialty from Nagoya she hadn't eaten in months.

When the phone started buzzing in her purse, Sachiko grabbed it and turned it off. She couldn't say what had happened, but she was resolved not to talk to the man ever again. Too uncomfortable, the thought made her cringe.

Moments later, she pulled away from the curb. Away from the restaurant, the date that derailed and made her feel bad, to find a place that served Mexican food. Or perhaps she would keep on driving, farther and farther, until she finally reached the coastline, the expanse of the sea. She would head on into the water and across the whole clumsy ocean, past Hawaii and the Bonin Islands and across the International Date Line, all the way to the shores of Japan and then on to the town of Nagoya. She would meet up with friends for dinner and then drink and sing songs at karaoke, an evening of sweet familiarity.

As the rain started coming down, a mass of water enclosing the car and hammering against the windows, the wipers unable to manage and offer any sort of view, Sachiko sensed something well up inside her, an anger so deep it was frightening. She suppressed the emotion, swallowing it like a dark fruit. A deep breath before the journey, then she moved back in her seat and turned up the music on the speakers, mouthing the words of the song.

She hoped that the rain wouldn't stop, not until she had reached Nagoya.

Smoke in a Blameless Language

THE ROOM WAS small and left nowhere for the smoke, the result of three packs of cigarettes the men had finished between them. The ministry asked them not to use the facilities, the smoking lounge on the fourteenth floor, as their work was considered classified, and it was feared they might let secrets slip. Not hardly, mused Hayden, not now. The place for secrets was Southeast Asia—where the Americans kept raining bombs so that the dominoes wouldn't fall—not this island enjoying its peace.

The 1970s in Japan, the time Mishima never saw after committing his ritual suicide, would come to be known in history as the best time to be Japanese. The phoenix had risen and dusted off the old wings, then soared to its own surprise to new heights of happy materialism.

The room had a little screen and projected there was a movie, an eight-millimeter reel from a distributor that was well-preserved for its age. A Hollywood noir from the 1940s, it was set during the American occupation.

As plumes of smoke curled up from their cigarettes through the light from the humming tripod, the men watched as an American actor arrived in a black-and-white Tokyo, a scene actually not shot in Japan. The rear projection of houses and street scenes looked staged even for the time, an arrival that never happened in a mythical foreign land, which for Americans had been Japan. Hayden had liked the movie, had seen it as a little kid at a matinee screening back in Montgomery, back in the days when audiences dressed up for the movies. On this screen it looked awfully dated, a throwback to another age, churned out in a matter of days on a backlot in Culver City.

"I helped kick it around," the actor snarled on the screen, meaning Tokyo during the war. "And if it happens again, I'll do the same thing."

Nakamura paused the projector, sucking his teeth. He was in his mid-twenties, well-groomed and of graceful carriage, with honest eyes and a close-clipped mustache that matched his long and smooth sideburns. His eyes on the screen, he shook his head no. This too wouldn't do, not at all.

Hayden nodded agreement. He had seen the declassified footage of the American bombings of Tokyo, the carnage of Operation Meetinghouse that had caused the canals to boil in the fire and burned alive several thousand civilians. "Kick around" was a poor choice indeed, a candidate for revision.

"How about *kowasu*—to demolish?" Nakamura shook two cigarettes from a pack. "More serious. And more gravitas."

"A bit harsh," Hayden frowned. "A bit too much empire."

Not as empire as a firebombing, Nakamura mused. With an air of resignation, he took a black notebook out of a drawer and made some notes in quick Japanese. Every change needed ministry approval, then he would go to a nearby studio and burn the new lines on the negative.

"What goes in there?" Hayden nodded at the notebook. "More terms for blowing to smithereens?"

"Just my own record. Our work still evolves."

The man is brilliant, each of them thought. Only sometimes, he doesn't get it.

Immersed in their work for hours as they watched scenes again and again, the two men checked the speech of the actors, the meanings and time that it took to read characters on the screen, then discussed with a solemn focus about cadences and respect. They both loved movies, even the strange ones, and it was out of this ardent love that had evolved through the years of their lives—the devotion of connoisseurs who had skipped classes, homework, and dinners to watch dreams unfold in the dark, alone in the theaters of their youth—that they wanted them to be better, to endure in a better version and delight future generations. The world of dreams was a place they took seriously, perhaps more seriously than the world around them, and with the ardor of men sharing a passion, and with the competition of scholars working at happy peak expertise, committed to getting it right as they parsed each obscure connotation, they kept awing and topping each other as masters of a foreign idiom.

"May I ask something, Hayden-san?"

Nakamura paused as they left the building, a government complex in Kasumigaseki. It was after midnight, the air warm with spring.

"Americans cannot see this? You see it only when we point it out?"

Hayden thought to find the right words. "We didn't think that there was a problem. We made movies for the times, for Americans. The people who paid for the tickets."

A gray Mercedes pulled up to the curb, the driver ordered by phone. Nakamura took a deep breath.

"A note came this morning, a change at the top." He seemed flustered. "Azusa Honda, the head of Central Liaison. She will supervise and report to the PM."

"Any grief?"

"More changes may be requested, more tweaks. I hope she won't make things difficult."

"It's starting to feel like too many cooks. Not sure we can make everyone happy."

"Also, her husband has asked to meet you. A welcome from the business community."

"The husband?"

Hayden was still in shock as the car door closed automatically.

As they moved to the prefectural highway that would take them to Kamakura, passing office towers and government buildings, the moat of the Imperial Palace and the cherry trees overhanging the banks in their bloom, he saw again how the place had changed. Some canals had made way for new highways and yet traffic was somehow worse, the air thick with motor exhaust from newly affordable cars. Since the Olympics eight years ago, the whole country had poured into Tokyo and the housing boom never ceased, making the city a metropolis of the world.

The small Subaru, discreet as a shadow, hung on to them through each curve. A Japanese move, less to watch him than his reaction to being watched, tailed at the behest of the ministry. Hayden leaned back in the seat, his features in thought.

Liaison meant interference, new stakeholders in the mix. The short men in belted coats and checkbooks of nervous nationalism, eager to assert themselves. The whole mission cast into peril by a woman he had abandoned, the husband who now wished to see him.

Twelve years ago, on a morning in Shinagawa, the air had been soft as well. The streets lay empty in the humid heat that would last for another month.

She had clutched the frame of the entrance, her face turned to anguished ice. Her shock came as muttered curses, her eyes dead as the message sank in because Hayden was leaving the country and thus, by extension, the rest of her life. They had agreed to put minds aside and let bodies speak for themselves, but then as feelings started to develop and the American morphed from an extra who complimented a marriage to a contender who might substitute the husband, the American had gotten cold feet just at the moment his studies ended. And so, on the summer morning twelve years ago, and then over and over, replayed in their minds like a scene in a movie they wished that they could revise, Azusa Honda had vowed to destroy him, then slammed the door in his face.

The Mercedes stopped at the house, a wooden frame near the beach. Hayden stepped through the narrow entrance, the sliding door after the *genkan*, then pulled the curtain in front of the bath and drew water in the wooden tub. The house was traditional Japanese, the same he had rented last time. Unchanged like a dream, he thought, smelling the pine in the walls.

After a soak that warmed him down to his bones, he settled in for the night with a drink. He put a handful of ice cubes into a glass, poured three inches of Santori whiskey, then swilled the mixture around in the glass to cool and dilute it. Outside in the dark, the waves lapped against the shore as though beating the passage of time. Persistent like the sighs of history, the conscience of atomic scientists.

Long ago, he had made a decision that had changed the rest of his life. The bridges lay ashed, like fictions on a yellowed map. The imperial order was to forget, as if the past were nothing but smoke.

The story of Porter Thelonious Hayden, the man who understood Japan more deeply than any scholar hailing from the West, began with his first arrival in Tokyo. It was springtime in 1960—a time when all sorts of changes were in the air. Emerged from the wartime rubble and having endured the American occupation, the Japanese had rebuilt their country and ushered in a new era. Tokyo was roiled by resistance, the rejection of a security pact that meant more dependence on America. Streets were blocked with protests as blossoms falling from cherry trees mixed in the air with leaflets, released from the hands of youth on the angry rooftops of revolution. A new sort of spring snow, summoning a revolt.

As Hayden had ventured out to the Imperial Palace and then

nearby Hibiya Park, past the music pavilion and gardens with blossoming tulips, a mass of students and teachers and labor unionists came stomping along the paths holding banners, chanting away in a language he had previously known only from books.

"*Ampo Hantai! Ampo Hantai!*"

They are speaking in Japanese, Hayden thought. The Japanese language is real!

The first American to be allowed at the venerable Tokyo University, Hayden drew from obsessive discipline as he set out to master the language. He immersed himself down to his soul, the one-in-a-million American who could think like a Japanese. His studies extended to tea and bohemian cafés, and it was then on one of his roams, at a poetry night in Shinjuku, that he ran into Azusa Honda.

It was late when she came onstage, dressed in a mauve kimono that marked the social class she inhabited. Her small shape erect, a notebook in her gloved fingers, she had read in a stilted voice that put Hayden in mind of kabuki. The poems were veiled in metaphor yet the images of devastation—a stroller melted into pavement, old men stumbling, howling out of their minds—had alluded to Hiroshima and the day of the atomic bomb. Under muted lights, Azusa read with deep concentration to an audience of students who couldn't follow her old-fashioned tanka, the way she parsed syllables into verse as though embalming them for the ages. Hayden was struck by her aloneness. A woman in middle age and her elegant, arcane poems, unable to reach the audience before her. She had embraced herself as a snob, a jewel hardened with pride. The world was asked to adjust.

Passing Hayden on her way out, Azusa gave him a short, strange look that only later he read as a challenge.

"Your tanka is masterful." He searched her dark eyes.

"You looked absent. I feared that I may have bored you."

"Not at all, it was really a treat."

"You would like to hear more another time?"

A week later, they were in bed—a surprise on both ends. An invite to the mansion in Shinagawa and a supper of Japanese steak and red wine, then Azusa made a calm proposal as Hayden listened with widening eyes. He agreed without trusting his luck, then, after more rounds of red wine, was led to the boudoir. There, without further ado, she received the thing she had asked. An amour from the West, rare and fabled, the first American she could respect since her childhood during the occupation. An inner need seemed to pull them together, a hunger to fill an emptiness they both always had inside them. They couldn't explain the allure, not in mannered conversations over dinner, but if a bedroom can serve as a transport, a means to become a person one cannot be anywhere else, not with anyone else, then Hayden and Azusa Honda had pushed all the fantasy buttons. Her legs in the air, short and strong, her skin like the snow on mountains in Yamagata. Hayden was on her, unthinking, the eyes of the spouse on his back in the dark.

The next day was Emperor's Birthday, a national holiday in Japan. A mild morning, the air filled with the smell of the sea. The schoolgirls were twittering birds as they skipped down the slope in their uniforms, rushing to cram school with backpacks rattling.

Hayden walked down to Enoshima and had lunch at a sidewalk café, where a little boy, after seeing him, gave a scream and ran to his mother. Hayden smiled at the fear of foreigners, then paid and returned to the house. He loved being alone with the work, a language that still intrigued him and had immeasurably changed his life, that made him lose and then find himself in a larger, more meaningful world. His face in a solemn focus as the sun passed above the sea, he was thumbing through faded dictionaries and reading with Japanese eyes, smoking absently in search of terms that held no offense to his hosts. A matter of tone and semantics, of nuance and connotation. Because some words invite their friends.

As a man from Selma, Alabama, where the people will make

great efforts to keep up the public peace, Hayden fathomed the Japanese the way only a Southerner could. The importance of social approval, the obsessiveness over appearance that stemmed from the fear of the side eye, the judgment of other people—all of this Hayden knew from back home and recognized in the Japanese. He knew the sentimentality: the grandeur that was the past and the rituals that had kept their meaning, the shameful defeat in a battle of honor. He knew the sting when the war was used to pull rank, because Americans love a winner, and they remember forever who lost. The losing side has to adapt, to live with a new sense of self that may leave them starved for respect. And so, humbled from wounded pride and sensitive to how things looked, the South and Japan were polite to each other.

He spent evenings at the house, overlooking the sea. All was silent on Enoshima, the graves on the hillside like flowers. Unlike the soft, sandy beaches near Mobile, the sea here was mindful of the ages. A mass shimmering in the moonlight, the numberless schools of waves were lapping against the shore.

A mutilated cable, an offense remembered. An intentional misunderstanding.

When the phone rang just before midnight, he knew immediately who it was. She always rang late at night, at home in a darkened room.

"Are you alone, Porter-san?"

"Of course. Aren't you?"

Her soft laugh surprised him. He expected hard feelings, an armor of ice and resentment, not the old rapport that it signaled. He realized with a shock how much he had missed her.

"How is the house? Still the same? I wondered if you needed more space. Our houses are small for Americans."

Hayden pictured her in the mansion, enveloped in opulence of her choosing. Was she perched on the bed in her silk, the large telephone in her lap as she absently played with the cord?

He had woken up in that bed on mornings etched into his memory, Azusa beside him sleeping, the sheets on her small, firm breasts. How unlike a Southern woman, he thought, the way emotions were kept under wraps until finally they were alone and her cold eyes warmed from inside, until the doors of the bedroom were locked and another person, a woman alive with desire, emerged in between the sheets and surprised him with sudden needs. He found blood on his back sometimes, crusted and dark, drawn from her nails on his skin.

"Kamakura has beautiful light," he said. "I don't remember the view like this."

"You were young back then. Other things held more interest."

"How is Mamoru?" Hayden thought he should ask, though she never mentioned the husband. A banking tycoon and his wife in a marriage that was a mystery to most people, the Hondas were part of the Ginza set, a group of conservative socialites whose banquets and cherry-blossom viewings were featured in gossip pages. As most childless couples in Japan, they were rumored to be desperately unhappy in a union of fading convenience, a view neither of them cared to dispel. More than anything, they secretly feared being normal and seen as regular Japanese.

"I suppose he is in Osaka." Azusa sounded indulgent. "A meeting with a new board, which means he is taking them golfing."

"Still in Abiko on the weekend? Selling real estate in between swings?"

"The irons are in the hallway, he grabs them on his way out. More convenient that way, I suppose."

A pause on the line weighed openness and politeness. Hayden listened to the sound of the waves as they washed in and out on the shore.

"The work has progressed? You have all that you need?"

"Nakamura is great, a huge help. He speaks English like an American."

"The best that we have." Azusa was pleased. "I know you can be demanding."

"The screening is still on next week? I suppose we are almost wrapped."

"I like that expression. Wrapped. So final and neat, reassuring. So much has changed in Japan, it all seems like a massive whirl."

"I've been invited to see Mamoru. A hello from the chamber of commerce."

Her laugh pearled, just almost. "Please say hello from his wife. No doubt he'll discuss new directions, his favorite topic."

"I doubt it was his idea, having me back in Tokyo?"

"In a way, he was overruled." Her voice no longer indulged. "Mamoru loves money and has his own passions, but in the end, he remains a child. I never saw what he needed to prove."

"You've seen the work? I am wondering—"

"I have final approval, reporting to the PM. There must be no misalignment."

Another pause, but he couldn't say what it weighed. The sea outside was a poem, seamless and without message.

"Sweet dreams, Porter-san," she said finally. "We shall meet again soon. I want to see the way you have changed."

The phone clicked silent.

The entertainments remained the same, yet the audience felt somehow different. A dissonance, a matter of tone that was hard to explain—in fact, it was hard to perceive unless your ears were attuned to the notes. The Japanese loved Americana, the cowboys and Indians and soldiers from the 1950s that were shown on TV and in theaters, yet when the plots involved Japanese characters, they found slights and stereotypes in abundance, a condescension leaving a taste that was sourer than pickled plums. If, as they say, films were the language of dreams, they now had to change for the dreams to work. A committee was formed to choose titles, a list of classics set in Japan that were deemed culturally or aesthetically significant, and then soon someone remembered Hayden, a man steeped in their culture and language, a man able to hear with ears that were not of his native birth.

The mission was grandly ambitious, the first of its kind in the world. To change forever the movie ways in which Americans talked to the Japanese.

Indeed, Hayden was the perfect match. Ambition had sent him from Alabama to the eminent hallways of academe, a scholarship at Harvard University, where he won accolades as a Japanologist. It was there, earning a doctorate and penning papers that would later shape government policy, that he learned about rank in America. He impressed audiences with his insights on shogun speeches or the symbolism in poems by Kawabata, catching depths of nuance and meaning inaccessible to other scholars. All along, though, he feared he might not belong as a Southerner in the Ivy League, a rube who might lose respect the moment his accent betrayed him. It was the awareness of rank—the doubts that continued to haunt him even seated at the chosen table, forever proving his worth—that he recognized in the Japanese.

They were intuitive people, like Southerners, ever wary of being belittled or seen as a little slow. They could smell respect, the exact amount they were getting, and they had seen the adventurous Americans who arrived in Japan and took what they needed, then left in the dead of night. With Hayden, they sensed a difference. The careful way he would listen, the thoughtful look on his face. As proud as a Japanese, he had humbled himself before them by learning their complex language, and in turn, they adored him, embraced him as one of their own. His skills were unmatched in both countries and the prestige he gave to the project, along with the approval of his employer, the US Department of State, made the Japanese spare no expense to have him assist with the movies. As the war in Vietnam ground on and America needed Asian allies, Tokyo was keen to cement a partnership that would see them through the

Cold War. Their faith in Hayden was boundless; the feed to his ego never ceased. Together, it was dreamed on both sides, they would make diplomatic history.

"Welcome to Tokyo—or welcome back, I should say. A great honor and pleasure."

A firm awkward handshake, a tension as their eyes met. Slim and youthful in a turtleneck sweater and a casual tailor-made suit, Mamoru Honda, though shorter than Hayden, had a supple build from his exercise on the links. Behind fashionably rimless spectacles, his face was strikingly handsome and tanned from outdoor activities, even features and deep dark eyes that probed Hayden with childlike bluntness.

"The pleasure is mine," Hayden said coolly.

"You must find the city much changed. The '60s seem so far back, we almost wonder if there was electricity."

"It was marvelous, actually," Hayden said. "And marvelous what you have done with it."

The office was spacious and modern, certainly by Japanese standards, up in a tower in Marunouchi with a view of the Imperial palace. Mamoru stood by the window, looking down on the tiny specks that moved in the park-like expanse. Unlike his wife, he was dressed in the latest fashion and spoke with a youthful idiom.

"The emperor just returned from Europe, a smashing success and welcome. Our standing has so much improved since the chance to hold the Olympics." Mamoru smiled thinly at his own reflection, as if to confirm the smashing success.

"I must admit, it is nice to be back."

Hayden sat down and took out his cigarettes, then reached for the granite tabletop lighter. He kept wondering why he was summoned as his host volubly thanked him for coming, the work he was doing for the nation.

The man he remembered was insecure, a little too eager to please. A scion from a family of bankers, Mamoru had misspent most of his youth in the pursuit of libertine thrills, a row of scandals involving starlets and hushed payments from family lawyers, until marriage to the older Azusa had called for a straightening out. Moving from finance to media commentary, he had recently published a book, a volume of essays on patriotism that had landed well with conservatives. *Dawn of Pride* was a hymn to the nation full of fiery unabashed prose, making a case for restoring honor as a new economic force.

"I appreciate the welcome, especially . . ." Hayden made a small awkward gesture. "I read your essays on the flight over. Some excellent points there indeed."

"I was trying to show a new path. A new purpose for an ancient nation." Mamoru looked flattered and excited. "There were questions that had to be settled, about the future, the sort of country we want to be. The communists and the student protests, these people rejected everything without offering more than a dream. Thankfully, things have calmed. We are poised to achieve new greatness and have learned how to handle the burden. Indeed, we have outgrown our teachers."

Hayden studied the handsome face, the smooth black hair and the sideburns groomed in the latest fashion. The man who had shared his wife, a man he hadn't considered a rival.

"Are you a nationalist?" he asked abruptly.

"You mean, do I think the Yamato race is superior?" Mamoru drew on his menthol cigarillo, a brand that most nationalists would abhor. "Of course, I don't. My school never sang the national anthem, never visited any shrines to remember the dead of the war. We have been humbled in many ways."

"The things you write, though. The reactionaries must love them."

"Let me ask something, Hayden-san. A question I have had for years. Can we Japanese be as proud, can we ever like ourselves as much as you like America? I mean, are we allowed this? I am serious, because that is my aim."

"It's not your words so much as how people hear them. A nation divine, the emperor at the center. Then things get messy."

"How do you mean?" Mamoru looked up. "Messy like Vietnamese villages, the farmers on fire?"

The sudden tension, the silence that filled the office as Mamoru kept holding his gaze, sent Hayden back to the Shinagawa mansion. An opulent master bedroom, murmuring in the dark. A strange and unusual arrangement, a couple and another man.

Some men attempt to set certain rules as they embark on a reckless venture, in hopes of retaining a sense of control. Mamoru had asked to ignore him, the fact that he ever existed or had feelings that could be hurt. Nothing indicated that he was there, in the bedroom with them. He entered unseen, never meeting or even acknowledging them as his focus was the American, the man who had charmed his wife with his old-fashioned Southern manners, his love of poems that most Japanese couldn't read. A silhouette in the dark, Mamoru listened for any sound that suggested what they were doing. A moan or a sigh, a rustling of sheets—whatever could feed the movie that played silently in his head. He never wished to be able to know, to see his wife with another man and be humiliated in the open. It would have chilled his delight in an instant.

Mamoru turned, facing Hayden. "There is something I need to tell you, a matter about your mission." He paused, then chose his words carefully. "The men who sponsor you, they are part of another generation. A most honorable generation, mind you, no matter what some may say. Only their hearts are still with the past now, and you could say they are making an investment. The films they chose are about the last war."

"And what, may I ask, is your investment?"

Mamoru smiled thinly. They both knew what was now discussed, why in fact the meeting was called.

"I'm not interested in old movies. The whole poking around in the past, to see if it comes up different. As for your question, I invest in the future. My work and the Japanese nation—as well as, of course, my family."

His gaze simmered behind the spectacles, the resentment of former students in the old lecture on Western values. The lecture had once been useful and the students eager to learn, but it had gone on year after year, a monologue that never knew the extent of its own paternalism, a lecturer who never minded that the students were always quiet.

Hayden rose with a new respect. "I'll get back to work, not to waste any of your taxpayer money. See you next month at the screening?"

"So glad we had a chance to meet. And do enjoy your stay in Japan."

Somewhere in the heart of the hours missing him, Azusa Honda had resigned herself not to poison her American lover. No reappraisal or mood of forgiveness allowed her at last to let go; the matter was purely of self-preservation. She had exhausted herself hating Hayden, which in the end, she explained to herself, only showed that her love was still burning. To get over him meant to stop serving him, to stop going to Kamakura and stare at the shuttered house, listening to the waves as she sat on the beach for hours. It meant also to forsake resentment, the dream of seeing him convulsed in agony until he coughed up a dark red foam and begged on his knees to be spared.

It was hard to let go of the dream. She had cherished the thought of the foam.

In a society marked by restraint and the muting of personal needs, sometimes women are at their most honest when they are acting most recklessly selfish. Beyond caring about approval and appearance, or even hoping for eventual forgiveness. However, the island that was home for Azusa wanted women more pleasant than honest, and it most certainly wouldn't let them be selfish. And so, in gossipy newspaper ink and ramen shop judgments from Hokkaido all the way to Kyushu, Azusa Honda had paid a price for stepping eagerly into scandal.

The arrangement with the American, the fluidity of the Honda marriage that was equally modern and traditional and had idle minds running wild, was told to the press by a spinsterish maid. The public was thrilled, then scandalized, if persistently keen to hear more, and the shockwaves of the affair smashed all hopes for Azusa and higher office, any meaningful public career beyond fussing around in Liaisons. Of course, experiments happened in certain circles and in the freewheeling 1960s could be reconciled with Japanese mores. But Azusa Honda? The icon of Tokyo snobbery with her brand of sophistication, engaged in a sordid affair with her millionaire husband watching? The husband himself could hardly believe it.

"It wasn't healthy, the whole experiment." Mamoru shook his head thoughtfully. "The mere notion. I don't think you could hate me like that."

They were perched in the winter garden in the warmth of the evening sun, reminiscing and sipping sake in a moment of rare tranquility. Before them on a low table was a small lemon torte.

"You spoiled me, I have to admit." Azusa served up the torte. "But then it might be why we are married. Why you indulge me when I am strange."

"An American—what were we thinking?" Mamoru affected an air of disgust. "It was different from what we do, of course."

"I enjoy what we do . . ." Her voice sounded absent. They hadn't mentioned the affair in years, never aimed to repeat what they privately called a mistake.

At an earlier time in their marriage, the Hondas looked up to Americans. What was the secret, they thought, to their sparkling allure? What made them larger than life and speak to the world with an inborn confidence no Japanese could hope to possess, first as occupiers after the war, then as shiny superior models setting trends in movies and magazines? In the feverish minds of the Hondas, American lives had an effortless cool on a grander, more theatrical scale, promising riches unobtainable in Japan. Eventually, this had made them curious about American ways of making love.

Azusa had made the suggestion, first on a whim, then as part of a teasing challenge to the permissiveness of her husband, a man who had never learned to say no to his older wife. They were further seized by the notion, a belief common among Japanese, that each pursuit has a mastery of form, a particular technique or manner in which a thing is most pleasingly, most consummately done. And thus, the Hondas had turned to Hayden, to be apprenticed for a mastery in bed.

"It is hard to keep marriage exciting," Mamoru sighed. "But, I never saw much in Hayden. He seemed strange, not cheerful like other Americans. A bit lost, like he wanted to be Japanese."

"It is past, never mind him now." Azusa stared at the torte like a deepening sexual mystery.

"And you are sure that revenge isn't needed? Forgiveness is not your forte. I know forgiveness."

"Hayden is loyal, as long as he thinks he is in control. And I'm too old for malicious games."

"Indeed—though I shouldn't call it a game." Mamoru looked at Azusa, eyes probing behind the glasses. "And I have known you to be malicious."

Azusa remembered the pain that had followed her for many years. The part of her that had softened and been eager for Hayden's approval, the part she resented most and that had needed to seek revenge.

The following night, after working late, Hayden was dropped off back at the house to find an envelope on the front steps, delivered there by a messenger. The monogrammed card was embroidered with blossoms and wrapped with a small silken ribbon.

> Your voice sounds deeper. I am intrigued.
> Dinner at our house on Sunday?

—A

A soft wind came along from the sea, schools of waves moving on the shore.

The garden was still as massive, even for this part of town, still as hushed behind the old stone wall as he remembered from years ago. The same creak in the roofed wooden gate with the Honda name on a plaque, the same rustle in the neatly trimmed hedges, the bamboo shading the pond and the stone lantern. There were clouds in the sky yet no hint of rain as Hayden moved past manicured cedars to the entrance of the modern mansion. An odd feeling overcame him, the past tugging at his insides.

A new houseboy answered the chime, handsome in hakama pants. He led Hayden down a narrow hallway and then through the spacious salon, past the sleek earth-toned furniture and artisan chests from Kyoto, the coffee table that had cost a fortune because Noguchi made only one. As always, Hayden paused at the portrait of Nobosuke Honda, a minister in the wartime cabinet who looked sternly at fading fortunes.

"You have grayed on the sides. Why so serious?"

Azusa looked down from a gallery, measuring him with small eyes.

Her skin was the same, unblemished, the pride was still in her face. The hair was short, the style a concession to age that must have been coaxed by a stylist. Her elegance was stressed by the kimono, a subtle wisteria pattern that clung to her shape as she swished down the wooden stairs. She bowed deeply upon reaching Hayden, a decorum hiding the intimacy they had shared in the house in the past.

"Welcome back, Porter-san. So glad you could join us."

Her eyes were ovals under thin arched brows. Behind them, things waited and watched.

As he studied her from behind on the way to the dining room, the shape of the patterned kimono revealed the changes in her body.

The softening of middle age had made her step slower, a little more measured, yet like a feline beyond her youth, she still moved with impeccable grace. Hayden wondered what was planned for dinner.

Mamoru, elegant in a white dinner jacket and what seemed to be leather boots, called his name in affected delight, then rushed over for a handshake. He motioned at a man at the table, who rose and bowed with silver-haired gravitas.

"Undersecretary Shimura," said Mamoru. "Another sponsor of your excellent mission."

Seated at the end of the table, Hayden experienced again the changes that occurred to him in Japan, the way that the country allowed him to be comfortable in his skin. To his hosts, Alabama wasn't poverty or a mess of mean race relations, it wasn't hicks who thumbed musty bibles to the embarrassment of the coasts. Instead, his hosts charmed him by admiring new Bermingham funk and the sublimeness of Tennessee Williams, the great artists his state had produced, then expressed fondness for barbecue chicken and interest in fried green tomatoes.

As the mistress served the tempura that was made by a chef in the kitchen, Hayden watched with intrigue how the Hondas interacted, how Azusa, often bossy with men, now deferred to her younger husband. As the daughter of diplomats in Yamanote, the area west of the Imperial Palace where the privileged had lived for centuries, Azusa knew that men could have deeper, more enjoyable conversations when they ignored the women at the table. Her schooling at Oxford and Kyoto University, the exchange year at the Sorbonne where she took courses in history and comparative literature, had equipped her to hold her own in discussions anywhere and with anyone, yet she would offer no questions or thoughts as the talk moved to Tokyo Marine and Kansai Electric Power, the sort of old-fashioned Japanese stocks that were owned by conservatives like the Hondas. Her face seemed absent, a mask of politeness.

"Our guest must be bored," she said after dessert. "It is time for his gift."

She rose and swished out of the room, then returned with a small wooden case embellished with formal characters. Stopping alongside Hayden, she opened the case and displayed an expensive bottle. A decade later, she still remembered his favorite whiskey. Keeping the label face up, she poured a glass from a height with the grace that mesmerized Hayden. Her eyes on the liquid amber, she held the bottle at belly and neck in a manner denoting deference, standing so close he could sense her warmth.

"The ministry is impressed by your work." Shimura seemed genuinely pleased. "The new versions, so much improved. We cannot wait to see *Sands of Iwo Jima*."

Hayden looked up, alarmed. He hadn't known this was on the list, a mean piece of propaganda that should hardly appeal to his hosts, no matter the efforts of polish. Was there a misunderstanding? What did the ministry think they were doing?

"The changes are mainly in tone," he addressed Shimura. "We take off some of the edges. In essence, the stories remain."

A pause of surprise, then Shimura made a thin, puzzled laugh. "Too modest, Hayden-san, much too modest. Surely, your work makes a difference."

As dinner came to an end, Hayden excused himself for the washroom. Alone in the hall, he stood listening into the house. A mad impulse struck, then memory guided him to the wooden staircase, up the stairs to the private quarters and past the locked study, the bathroom in marble, redolent with roses—all the way to the master bedroom. He closed his eyes and took a deep breath. Almost soundlessly, he opened the fusuma sliding doors.

A Japanese-style bedroom, a futon with small hard pillows, tatami and pinewood walls that were so plain they must have cost a fortune. Hayden was stunned how the room had changed to where even the smells were new. Something touched him about the arrangement, something earnest about the intimacy that still seemed unsure of itself. For the first time, he sensed the damage he once had done to the marriage.

Mamoru was part of the darkness, as quiet as the small framed woodblocks and the vintage clock on the wall, unable to reach or affect them. His invisibleness was the key, the thing that allowed them to hurt him. One night, a sigh had rippled the sheets, the hauteur erased from her face, then a gasp of revolt from the chair and feet rushing across the tatami. The fusuma shut with a slam, the shock of the line they had crossed. Azusa had called the following day, asking Hayden in roundabout terms if he could imagine a life with her.

"I thought I might find you here."

Suddenly, she was by his side. Rising on velvet slippers, she slid the door open for Hayden to enter. "We have made a few changes," she whispered.

"The old woodblocks . . ."

"I remember you liked them. Mamoru wanted something different, more modern."

Shocked by the intimacy they had entered, he stepped with her into the bedroom, into the warmth of the past they had shared. Azusa moved to a table with flowers, a spray of lilies in a vase.

"Why did you come back, Porter-san? You didn't think we would meet?"

"To be honest, I wasn't sure it was safe."

Azusa nodded without emotion. "You were cruel a long time ago, but that is the past. I am glad you came, I know how much this work means to you." Her fingers absently touched the lilies. "The ministry has opened a post, a position that suits you. I am friends with the people in charge."

"I can see expectations are high. The screening is still next week?"

"Upon my approval, yes."

She fussed with the lilies, then picked up the sprayer. "So humid today, it makes everything soft." Her voice had become strangely hoarse, "More comfortable, perhaps, if you take off your shirt?"

In the silence that thickened, her eyes remained on the mist that slipped down the stems of the lilies. Her lips parted, a sheen of sweat on her neck.

A spell made Hayden unbutton, then shed the dark silken shirt. Azusa turned round to face him and for a moment they studied each other, wondering if what they saw and the things that were in the past should make them allies or enemies.

"No gray on your chest. The years have been kind to you." She moved closer, the kimono rustling. "Am I making you nervous?"

Her fingertips brushed his chest, thick with the tufts that shocked her the first time he had undressed. Hayden glanced at the pastel bed, the blood rushing to his groin. How much time was there?

Her fingers stopped, then Azusa turned, her hands smoothing the kimono. Her slippers swished out of the room in an exit too rushed to be rude, then Hayden was left alone, perplexed and no shirt.

The farewell was all reserve, unlike the last time he left the mansion. Mamoru watched behind rimless spectacles as his wife walked the guest through the garden, to where the Mercedes parked at the gate. Azusa bowed like an old acquittance after a reasonably pleasant dinner, then, with short, measured steps, she minced back down the path to the house and her younger, successful husband, the life that he had made possible.

Hayden sat in the leather seats, his mind ablaze in hot flames. He had seen Azusa act reckless, only now, the stakes were much higher and with age, she was harder to read. He realized that he feared her, the pull she had over his life at a time when her marriage seemed doomed. Might a final trespass, a shared night that was turning back time, end up saving or ruining the mission?

The Mercedes was passing a park where people sat under the cherry trees, eating and drinking and admiring the blossoms, while Hayden thought over his past and future, the shape of his mistakes to come.

A school of salmon looped through the aquarium, at times nearing the glass, then darting away, avoiding any attention that might get them sent to the kitchen. A hostess in a kimono had fussed with the tweed Hayden offered, draping and rearranging it on a hanger like a garment of priceless value. In the muted light in the room, Hayden looked at Undersecretary Shimura.

"Nothing doing." He stubbed out his cigarette. "It is beyond the scope of the mission."

Shimura regarded him like a fancy toy that wouldn't start, then the Cabinet Secretary, a man with a large oval face that was lined from a lifetime of committees, dabbed his mouth with a linen serviette.

"The term is offensive, you have removed it from other films. A minor ask, it appears."

"The scene is combat, some of the worst. It is how soldiers talk in a war." Hayden paused to sip on his sake.

Deep in the bowels of the Mitsukoshi department store, the restaurant had small private rooms that smelled of tatami and pinewood. From a speaker behind the panels plinked a shamisen from a Noh play. Three days before the screening, Nakamura had escalated an issue, and now here was expensive sushi and the kahunas making requests.

"Surely your boys had names for Americans, and much worse. It is what makes the whole thing authentic." Hayden sighed. "You don't use honorifics in combat, not for men trying to bayonet you. And yes, it is terribly offensive."

"We aren't asking for honorifics, mind you." The Secretary folded his napkin. "The times were of conflict, we understand. The term in question, however—we Japanese loathe it. Precisely the sort of thing that your work should redress."

"I understand you may have hoped for more, but you can't take an American movie and then tweak it to tell your own story. If you want that, you should make your own movie."

Hayden put down his chopsticks, looking straight at his hosts. "I don't know how else to say this, but I didn't come here to sanitize history. Unless there is something I misunderstood."

A sense of station fell over the table. Hayden studied the men before him who had likely served in the war and seen combat themselves, perhaps willing to die for the emperor and trying to bayonet Americans. He wondered what it meant in their lives, the defeat and all that came after, the limbs and friends lost in death hell Okinawa in battles of utter nothing, nothing at all, then Hirohito surrender broadcasts and signatures on the *USS Missouri*, a strange-looking pipe blowing smoke in their faces and telling them how to live, how to think and vote in the way that was right, because daddy knows best and forever. What did it mean for the men before him, the for-nothingness traded for shame and having to master the language of the occupier, as they sat here in designer suits and clawed back to the dawn of pride?

"We do make our own movies. We are happy with them." Shimura smoothed the ends of his mustache as though pondering the meaning of happiness.

"Allow me to remind us respectfully of the original aim of the mission. It is to foster mutual respect through equality and understanding, thus ending forever the mindset of occupation that has marred relations between our countries." He paused for effect. "It would be unfortunate—in fact, disappointing to an extent as to suggest a suspension of the mission—if our readings somehow diverged."

"We sought you for the mission specifically," the Cabinet Secretary added. "A Harvard man, and then Todai, you had references from the Hondas. You have appeared on Japanese television." The last words were oddly emphatic, as if carrying unassailable credentials.

"We had faith in you and your skills. We trusted you would seize the moment, also in your career. Most of all, we trusted that you know us, that you can see with a new way of seeing. Now it appears though that you don't know us."

Hayden sat and endured the rebuke, the way he had learned from the Japanese. He knew the reaction from Azusa, who was equally thin-skinned and stubborn when it came to Japanese affairs, rejecting out of hand even the slightest criticism, in fact, clumsily changing the topic when her country was the least bit challenged.

Shimura cleared his throat awkwardly, then took the bottle of sake and topped off the cups on the table, in descending order of rank. Hayden suddenly noticed the envelope that seemed to have come out of nowhere. A tan rectangle with a tassel, swollen slightly in the middle, that emanated a strange energy.

The Japanese kept their eyes on their plates, solemn yet without focus. No one mentioned the move or its meaning as silence fell over the table, the envelope aching to be acknowledged. A struggle unfolded mutely, a wrestling for power and influence that lasted a helpless eternity, until the American rose for the bathroom. Upon his return, the waitress had cleared the table and the envelope had disappeared.

"Thank you so much for the meal." Hayden poured himself some more sake without offering any to the group. "May I suggest that we all move forward?"

"You won't reconsider?"

"You're overthinking this. You're obsessed with respect."

The Cabinet Secretary picked up the towel, nodding slowly as he wiped his hands. "Most nations worry what others think." His face was utterly expressionless. "Most nations, that is, except yours."

The meal ended with a formality that masked the unhappiness of the hosts. Nothing was certain, no steps were resolved as the men bowed a cold farewell. Hayden realized he had failed a test, that in the minds of the men that mattered, he no longer was a loyal man. A thin rain fell down on the Ginza, the blossoms sailing from trees and landing on dark wet streets.

Azusa called later that night. They discussed a few technical aspects that were safe and without any stakes, then Hayden was cut off mid-sentence.

"Shimura says you are being difficult. A small request was refused."

"I checked with State and it struck a nerve. They are drawing a line in the sand."

"It cannot be helped, I suppose. We should drop the subject." A long pause, then a whisper that crushed all resistance. "Can I meet you in Kamakura? No talk about work, I promise."

An hour later, she walked beside him, dressed in a dark silk robe and a wide-brimmed hat. They were tracing the steps of memory down the empty Enoshima colonnade, past the surf shops and a movie theater that showed samurai epics for pensioners.

"I've many questions, Porter-san." Azusa stopped short. "I often wondered what happened to you."

"Not much, I suppose." Hayden tried an ambiguous smile. "I came back stateside, confused about everything. An office job in Virginia, then moved to the Asia desk. I got teased as the guy who went native and thinks we can learn from the Nips. I sit at my desk, just watching the news, then write reports that nobody reads because only Vietnam matters. I feel sidelined. As if there is no more use for me."

He struck a match, then lit up a cigarette. "That is what happened. And now I'm back and refusing requests."

"Mamoru said you seemed lost. In fact, I always liked that about you."

"Some have mentioned a fear of commitment . . ."

"With American women too?"

"With everything," Hayden said. "With America."

"But perhaps you might live in America with a woman who is not from there?"

Hayden understood the point, which didn't mean he had a

response. "I don't know how to put it," he said. "I just can't seem to feel at home there."

Azusa looked suddenly morose. "I don't see what you mean. I enjoy living in Japan."

The moon shone through the limbs of the trees that were heavy with cherry blossoms. The air was warm, forgiving of lies.

Azusa had never known how to act like the sort of woman her countrymen could understand. And then Hayden had never asked. He didn't know why there were no children or what she needed from a man and marriage, the things she might see in her dreams now that the '60s were over, her wild years retired for good.

A path took them up a slope, where a shrine overlooked the seashore. They passed a gate that shimmered vermillion, then reached a basin made of rough stone. On the surface of the cleansing water floated the soft pink petals.

With measured, almost solemn moves, Azusa picked up the wooden ladle, then dipped it into the basin. Hayden held out his hands and Azusa ladled the water, rinsing the left, then the right, the liquid smooth on his fingers. Around them the air held the smell of the sea.

"You might as well know . . ." She rinsed her own hands, then replaced the ladle. "I never really fell out of love with you. I no longer think it is necessary."

The waves at the shore lapped in closer, insistent and helpless. At the shrine, the rich brown wood right before them, they shook the rope of the muted bell, then stood for a moment in prayer. As Hayden seemed ready to leave, Azusa got up on her toes and brushed petal dust off his shoulder, a maternal touch he hadn't seen.

"We shouldn't have come where we used to come. It makes memories sad."

"I didn't mean to . . ."

"It was my idea. To see what it would be like."

She took a breath when she entered the house, absorbing the

smells unchanged by the years of her absence. A sigh escaped from her lips as she entered the room and the past, putting her shoes where she used to put them on weekends unknown to her spouse. Her fingers brushed the fusuma, the sliding doors closing on secrets.

"It feels like before," she said, turning to Hayden. Her eyes were like dancing embers. The last week was a charmed consensus, the work smooth and fast. Perhaps they were keen to finish or perhaps they had less to defend; whatever was happening exactly, the notebook remained in the drawer as Nakamura accepted all changes. No mention of the Ginza dinner, not even in Hayden's reports, as they bonded in the gentle manner of company workers in Japan. They complained about the long hours and the crowded commuter trains, sharing smokes and even lunch boxes and joking how Japanese wives made treats that Hayden couldn't get at the stores. They even brought beer for each other the night they fixed two more wartime noirs.

One day, the entrance was clammed as a shell. Hayden stood in front of the projection room, staring at his useless keys. The ministry must have changed the locks. The guard bowed excessively, most awfully sorry indeed, mumbling something about clearance revoked. Anxiety washed over Hayden, the sting of exclusion he knew from the States. They couldn't do this, it wasn't possible.

A call at the mansion got him the houseboy, the Hondas were out and was there a message? Liaison gave him excuses that were evidently not the truth—a change of schedule, something about the funding—then a clerk referred him to Nakamura without answering any more questions. A sinking feeling returned to Hayden. The Japanese closing ranks and things slipping out of control. Not again, he thought, not with these stakes. The mission was too important, for himself and international affairs, and he couldn't just watch and do nothing as the ministry took the reins. A call back to Nakamura affirmed the worst of his fears.

"They took the movies, even my notes. It comes from the top, a new brief." Nakamura sounded embarrassed. "It makes no sense, things have been going well."

"The ministry dumped us. Thanks for your help—sayonara." Hayden swallowed hard. "Does this mean that I have been played? Did you all use me to get the goods, the American stamp of approval?"

"You know that's not true. And not fair."

"I'm done with cooperation. Good luck with your stupid farce." About to hang up, Hayden added with a sudden meanness he would later come to regret, "You're not American, Nakamura—not ever. You shouldn't fool yourself about that."

In the pause on the other end, Nakamura breathed without sound. "Your tone . . ." he muttered. "I'm not sure you have understood."

Hayden filed his report without mentioning Azusa, then rang up Spengler at Foreign Service. The liaison had many questions about the dinner in Ginza and what had been said at the table, then, calling the mission aborted and failed, he ordered Hayden to return posthaste.

"They're not getting it. And we don't get *how* they're not getting it."

"How do you mean, sir?"

"How the hell do you think I mean? They start the revision, it means we are out. This ain't history class in the South. I won't have it."

The remark cut deep, setting the old wound bleeding. Japan had remodeled Hayden, a rube from the rural South whose father had sold shoes on main street, into an expert on a global stage who consulted the Japanese. Now here as well he was sidelined, shunned by those he had meant to help.

The leather notebook, the notes in the drawer. What if, from the day he had started, they had worked at night somewhere else, changing every last revision and using instead their own titles, referring to Nakamura every time they had disagreed? Was the farce comprehensive, the treachery whole? Was he the ultimate foreigner stooge?

He had to attend the screening, assess the damage firsthand. Then leave the country and face a demotion, perhaps even dismissal at State. He had placed his bets on Japan, then lost everything to a woman scorned.

The Hibiya theater in Chiyoda was art deco from the 1930s, holding over a thousand seats that had sold out in less than a week. An assorted elite from politics, culture and finance was streaming through the carpeted foyer, admiring the chandeliers and the wide marble staircase, then filling the velvet seats that fanned out from the massive screen. Most women were dressed in kimono beside spouses in uniform suits, and as names were whispered through the rows, heads turned to the swish of starched clothing announcing a prominent entrance. The balconies and the floors were sold out, some even willing to stand in the back, and the formality of the event combined with a giddy anticipation, the excitement of serious adults who are waiting to see an old movie.

Hayden was in the rear, the sole foreigner in the crowd. It was late, his last night in Tokyo. His cases were packed, a morning flight taking him home to a rather uncertain fate. He was lost in his thoughts when Azusa appeared on the stage, a kimono hugging her figure with an elaborate silken sash. Alone in front of the audience, the way he had seen her reading poetry in Shinjuku, she was met with a muted applause.

After extensive expressions of gratitude—a nod to the men at the ministry, yet no mention of Hayden or Nakamura—Azusa explained the spirit of the project, the way it served to affirm a more modern identity for Japan. At this point, she concluded bowing deeply, the narratives of the past no longer belonged to one side.

Something about her talk, the way she evoked her ideas with an old-fashioned lofty diction, made him think of their time together. He had woken in an empty house, the sea calm and Azusa gone. The night had been different, not their best performance; she had not let him touch her hair.

Hayden realized with a shock that they wouldn't see each other again, that she was waiting for him to leave and exit her life forever. Had she aimed for this all along, ending his dreams of Japan with a few consequential calls? Had she needed an escalation, an even score no matter the damage, to be able to let him go?

The lights dimmed, the theater fell silent. The curtain creaked open to a screen that came magically alive, filling Hayden with the same enchantment he had known since he was a child watching matinees in Alabama. The dream had begun, he was ready. The music swelled with the solemnness of war into the clarion call of its time, the righteous trombones and trumpets evoking the best intentions as they summoned Americans to the fight, then it meshed with a drum-rolled march, the battle hymn of the Marines.

From the Halls of Montezuma
To the shores of Tripoli
We fight our country's battles
In the air, on land, and sea
First to fight for right and freedom
And to keep our honor clean

As the Americans on the screen started talking and Hayden leaned back in the comfortable seat, his eyes became fixed on the titles. He was curious, entirely calm. A sense of surrender, of boundless acceptance washed over him, unconditional in a way that no country could ever bestow. Letting go of the need to belong, his mind drifted away like a cloud, nationless in the sky above seas that were all connected, looking down on the earth without grievance.

The Summer We Watched All the Godzillas

THE SUMMER WHEN I was lost and spent nights watching these old movies, at times two or three in a row, was the hottest on record in Tokyo. The movies were part of her childhood, the monster nights at the orphanage, twenty girls and a small TV. As we sat in her room and watched whatever was on, Mutsumi would pick the next one as soon as the credits rolled. The movies all meshed together, especially as we neared dawn and it felt like they were being broadcast from a faraway spirit world.

We never sat next to each other but focused on the same story, and so in a way, we were always together. We were grateful that men had once squeezed into sweltering hot rubber suits and blown up miniature houses and power lines in orgiastic demolitions of Tokyo, so that now, decades later, we could enter the realm of Godzilla without having to think about our lives.

We kept them coming, the escape and the movies, because Mutsumi had trouble sleeping with those dreams in the middle of the night, a scream on her lips, then afraid to fall back asleep. *Henna yume*, she said in the mornings as she came shuffling out of the bath, destroyed from a night without sleep. On the bathroom door hung a poster in French, a quote from an obscure writer. *L'amour c'est être stupide ensemble.*

Sitting next to her on the floor, I tried hard to ignore the futon, the unmade sheets and the feminine smell. I couldn't look at her without having those thoughts. The hum of the electric fan made the room slow as a summer night, and slouched on the floor in her lounging pajamas, some crackers and beer at her side that were refilled on runs to the kitchen, Mutsumi would watch intently as Godzilla emerged from the sea and tussled awkwardly with a monster moth or a mutant crab out of its league, and she might look up and say, "Let's do Megalon next. I wanna see Godzilla and Megalon."

"You know they made a ton of these. Too many to watch them all."

"Yes, we can." Mutsumi downed her Asahi. "The night is young and I'm counting on you."

Any time we needed more monsters, we ran down to the DVD shop. They were round the clock, a basement emporium that was stuffed to the rafters with movies, a haven for soulless insomniacs who must come and rent one more thing. The clerk wore shades and dark leather, a hipster with a twisted past who sat there munching on gummies that he scooped up from a huge jar. We would grab our own snacks, then scan the shelves full of schlock from the '70s until Mutsumi found what she wanted. I thought Megalon was a joke, no matter how low the bar, but it was her apartment and DVD player, and so she decided. The movies were my ticket to her room, and I thought my best chance to score was to give her the run of the place. I was that age where men think they impress a woman by letting her choose a movie. Or maybe I wasn't that age, but a part of me thought that way. Mutsumi was just too beautiful. The legs of a dancer, the hair falling down her back. The high cheekbones and tasteful clothes, the deep eyes that warmed your soul!

She made it clear that nothing would happen. One Sunday

afternoon, unaware that she was awake, I ran into her in the kitchen as she was making a seaweed snack. Dressed in a robe and a towel turban, she stood there on naked feet and must have known what effect she had, then rebuffed my subtle advance.

"No hookups with roommates, I told you." She sounded stern, even though, to my recollection, no agreement like that had been made.

"I'm not into American men. You come here thinking you can make your pick, just take what you need and then leave. This isn't a toy store, *mon chère*."

"Who says that? Who are these people?"

I knew exactly who these people were, having heard tales of the foreigner clubs where the Americans whooped it up and made out like bandits in lust, enjoying shades of the occupation.

"You have so much to prove, it must hurt. Just *ponpon*." Her fist moved like a lusty jackhammer. "Not romantic at all."

"You should see for yourself what it's like. I mean, why are you always serious?"

"Because I've no sense of humor. None." She munched on the seaweed, her hair wet and glistening. "Everyone says that."

Embarrassing as it was to admit, my three months in Tokyo hadn't reaped much romantic excitement. The women I met made it clear they were looking for husband material, no foreign adventures, thank you. They were reserved, in fact, even guarded, as if they were warned in secret dossiers on the excesses of Western men and now saw me and seemed to think: *The last hundred guys who looked kind of like you got away with being total assholes. Let's see what we got here.*

My efforts netted one score exactly, which I'm not sure even counted. A makeup girl from the set, petite and morbidly shy, who had never dated a foreigner and admitted me to a small boudoir that looked like a shrine to anime. There were bunnies on posters, pajamas and pillows and then more bunnies on covers and sheets, and along with her constant giggles, I found it challenging to perform as though America was number one. Surely, he must have dreamed of one day meeting a man named Bugs.

The thing happened because she acknowledged me, unlike most of the staff of the show that had hired me for the season. A Tokyo job seemed exciting, especially as work was scarce and my twenties would soon be over. I was serious about acting and eager to give it my best, but the supposedly glamorous life and my hopes of a break in Japan had ended up disappointing. My role was a joke, so freed from all personality that a cardboard cutout seemed deep in comparison. I was asked to look cool and confident as I joined parties with views of Shibuya, invited by whom no one knew, a drink in my hand and the town at my feet as I yapped lines such as "Party down, boys and girls!"

"My god, the token American." Mutsumi rolled her large eyes. "No one knows him, no one has met him. You couldn't do better than that?"

"I didn't write the part. That was your people."

"Because we like mascots." Her long lips pouted. "Especially those from America."

Her sarcasm landed with ease, as if she were smarter than me and had practice. It was partly the reason why, when answering her ad for a roommate, I had agreed to share the rent equally even though her room was much larger. The apartment was so laughably small that her clothes were all over the place, the washing machine out on the balcony and shirts drying on racks in the bath. God knows what she did with her underwear.

As she worked nights and slept until noon, Mutsumi liked that our schedules were different and there was no waiting in front of the bath, no bottlenecks in the kitchen. She worked at a so-called *kyabakura*, an establishment where men pay money to talk to women whose real names they don't know. In dark velvet booths, a hostess in a slinky dress pours overpriced drinks while laughing demurely at a man's jokes and commiserating over his work—the long hours, the insufferable boss and the fawning that leaves scars on the soul—making him feel like an interesting person so he keeps ordering overpriced drinks.

The clubs stress with much indignation that, no, they're not *that* kind of place, which is both true and effectively without meaning. Nothing happens in the velvet booths or anywhere else in the club, but the odds of happenings elsewhere are discussed forever in terms veiled less than a hostess, who is dangled before the men like a juicy come-hither carrot. A perfect job for Mutsumi, all looks and great conversation.

Her status as a Tokyo demimonde never seemed to make her embarrassed, the way that you might expect from a modern, independent woman. The club was exclusive and paid very well, and since the one thing she seemed to hate was reliance of any kind, she could never be embarrassed by a job that allowed her to live her own life. Seeing me eat instant ramen and crackers and without money for going out, she said that for extra income, I could work as a host in Shinjuku, where a handsome foreigner pouring drinks could make even more money than she did. Not to say I was handsome, but hey. I almost choked on a cracker.

"Not for me," I scoffed. "Pretending that something might happen when I already know that it won't."

"Silly boy, it's the opposite. A host hooks up right away, to turn female guests into regulars."

"They come back?"

"All the time. Twice a week."

"But then how does the host keep their interest?"

"They're in love, silly. Hoping the host loves them back." Mutsumi smiled grimly. "An endless supply of overpriced drinks."

Born to a father she never met and a mom working minimum wage, she never saw herself as a victim but had learned not to wait for fairness or a white knight offering help. Most of her pay was spent on her passions, namely sushi and shopping for clothes and the rebuilding of Fukushima, her hometown prefecture in Tohoku. A tsunami had ravaged the coast there, leaving people stranded in shelters and children alone in orphanages, forsaken and with nowhere to go. Mutsumi made lavish donations, and each spring she would visit Minamisoma to join the memorials for the dead. The government honchos in Nagatacho, she said with the calm resignation that the Japanese have about their government, were too stupid and out of touch to help.

"You don't want to tell me about it?"

"There's nothing to say, not at the moment."

"I thought that is why we are meeting."

"We are going to see the French bookstore. To get maps of Paris."

A change of plans, evidently—and evidently, she wouldn't admit it. As open as she could be, Mutsumi was also guarded and grew restless when the world couldn't follow her. Did the world not know who she was?

Sitting next to her at Chez Jacques, an outdoor café with classical music and *croissant aux amandes* that could make women sigh, I sipped on my tea and looked out on the street, the trees lining the narrow sidewalk in front of the balconied facades, the flaneurs of Kagurazaka shopping for wine and kimonos or perhaps some imported cheese. The area was Tokyo at its best, a mix of samurai history and cosmopolitan chic.

Mutsumi loved all things French since she had seen *Les Misérables* as a little girl, awed that such sadness existed in the world. Her love of the culture extended to the men, which bothered me to no end. The sophistication and easy charm! The lightness that was infectious and could sweep up the dull Japanese!

I couldn't stand it. A Japanese crush I could live with, any Asian man, for that matter, but there was something about her liking French men that seemed like a personal challenge. I made it clear they were fervent sexists who treated women like the '50s were still a thing, that they had strangely strong thoughts about food and talked circles around you that made no sense while longing secretly to be Americans. Mutsumi just rolled her eyes.

"Let's get going. These paintings are awful, all wannabe French."

Behind the oversized sunglasses, her eyes mocked the art on the walls. A nymph in a stage of undress, cavorting with cherubs in clouds.

"I like wannabe French. It feels manageable."

Her dream to be a sophisticate made her seek out the old French classics, tomes by Colette and Simone de Beauvoir that she chose from a must-read-before-you-die list, then put aside, ever restless, after reading the first few pages. I should give her a novel, I thought—a tale of sophistication where nothing happens until the ending that will leave you forever depressed; where the men wear fashionable sweaters and sigh and say things like "Tell me you're happy, Eloise!" while the women smoke cigarettes of ennui, resenting their own petty selves, their own selfishness as they meet lovers in countryside inns because, deep inside, they fear emptiness in their soul and they are tired of running away. This kind of book might have struck Mutsumi. I'm not a fool without culture, mind you.

Leaving the bookstore, she held a copy of *Aimez-vous Brahms?* and three street maps of Paris. Two of the maps were a gift for Gaston, as though the name meant something to me. The plot thickened in front of my eyes.

"You didn't say you were going traveling."

"It's not that—I will live there. I need a change, can't you see? Tokyo is small and things never change, not for someone in my situation. Gaston has a friend with a club in Montmartre. They always need people, he says."

"You mean, you're in love?"

She made a sweet smile that said none of your business, then linked arms with me as we walked. "No worries, *mon chère*—we shall find you a nice new roommate. A Japanese girl who likes ponpon and makes you martinis after work."

I wasn't listening, shocked by the news. Mutsumi would leave because Tokyo was small, the way women leave men in French movies to escape from a haunted past. She was restless and out of step, and I think partly she had to keep moving because she survived where others had not. Now our days were suddenly numbered, the small, simple life we had made together. How much time was there? A month, a couple of weeks? And did it mean nothing that, the night before, exhausted and coming home late, she fell asleep in the glow of the television before Megalon even appeared, her legs curled up on the tatami, her face on my shoulder all lonely and me not moving an inch? I mean, do you think that meant nothing at all?

Of course, it was selfish. The American in the toy store who wouldn't go home empty-handed, who insisted on taking a memory or at least a small consolation. Nothing waited for me back home, not even dubbings or a ketchup commercial, and I thought Tokyo owed me that much.

"Not your moment," my agent said when I called for updates. "But Tokyo Disney might soon be hiring, shaking hands in the great parade. Of course, the costumes are hot in the summer."

Mutsumi liked me enough, I was sure. No reason at all why we couldn't have fun and stay friends.

On top of the hill was the communal bathhouse, a sento with a slanted roof that shaded the curtained entrance, and next to that was the geisha school.

A small, unassuming building at the end of an alley, the school had been there since the Edo period. Instructed by a famous geisha who was frequently on TV, the apprentices learned dancing and singing and how to pour sake at the neighborhood *ryotei*, the exclusive Kagurazaka restaurants where the guests need a personal invitation. Limousines parked in the streets at night like business panthers on hold, waiting for Tokyo elites who dined out the old-fashioned style.

The closest I came to a geisha was in our building. The apartment upstairs was sort of a changing room, a place for geisha to apply their makeup and arrange their hair in chignons, then tie the elaborate kimono and sash. Most weekends the wooden sandals would clatter down hallways and stairs as the geisha were leaving for work, yet no matter how alert I might be, I never reached the peephole in time to see them rush past our door. I tried hard, but those geisha were quick.

One night as the clatter faded, I spied a plastic bag through the peephole, dropped in a rush in the hallway. A lover of Japanese culture, I was dying with curiosity about the geisha and their effects. I stole out checking for neighbors, then snatched up the bag and opened it. An old hairband, a matchbook with two matches left. A pack of cookies, no cookies left.

American Oreos, snarfed by a Japanese geisha. Somewhere Kawabata turned in his grave, the culture sold down the river.

Mutsumi didn't like geisha because she thought that their lives were compromised, an insight she had arrived at after getting thrown out of geisha school. A geisha can use pretense the way Mutsumi did at her club, yet she had balked at the endless rituals that must be followed with rigor. Something to do with the tea pouring ceremony, the laying of the charcoal fire, which she dismissed as a pointless fuss.

"The teacher was dumb," she concluded. "Much better to be a hostess. Same racket, but better tips."

A week later she asked for a favor, if I could walk her home after work. Club Asia was close to our house and the streets were lit with neon, so I suspected she worried about a customer who might be turning into a stalker. She got messages all the time, men sending her raunchy notes or asking her out to play golf and take things to another level, even hackneyed haiku with confessions of love, which she thought was the worst offense. I helped gladly as I stayed up late anyway, coming home after hours of shoots where I stood there like a dumb American who was awed by the mysteries of the East.

I loved nightlife in Kagurazaka, the eateries tucked into backstreets that wound up and down the slopes, the small bars playing muted jazz to a handful of secret guests. The summer heat that would last until the first cool breeze in September turned the nights into their own events, everyone out and about and the restaurants full of laughs.

That night I was out on the street in a surfer shirt, passing students on dates and office workers bowing endless farewells on the sidewalk, when I came upon the wooden bathhouse, a house of gloom on top of a slope. It had been there since before the war, surviving the dreadful bombings and then constant urban renewal, and if neighborhood lore could be trusted, geisha came here in the early morning for a shower and soak after work. I stopped in front of the entrance, the sweat running down my shirt. I was meeting Mutsumi in an hour and I needed a place to think, to process what I had seen.

Behind the curtains and a latticed sliding door, an attendant with glasses and sweatpants manned a desk and collected admission. To make small talk as he counted my change, I asked him if foreigners ever had trouble following the sento etiquette, all the rules of a Japanese bathhouse.

"The Japanese make the trouble." He laughed, playing with hair in his ear. "The faucets left running, the towels all over the place. Their heads must be up in the clouds."

In the bathing area, a row of showerheads and low stools was in front of a mirrored wall, two large wooden tubs in the back. Behind a partition painted with a large peaked mountain, I heard women chatting and showers splashing, the whoosh of an ancient blow dryer. A group of geisha relaxing after work?

The tubs had two different temperatures, hot and so hot that a chef would think twice about tossing a lobster in there, afraid that the thing might dissolve. Two oldsters were sharing the boil, motionless and serene, yet no acknowledgment met my entrance, as if no tall naked stranger paraded in front of their eyes. I moved to the other tub, then slowly, mindfully, eased myself into the scalding heat. I leaned back with eyes closed in a manner of manly endurance, making idle waves with my hand as if musing about my life, the ephemeral nature of time. Soon my thoughts returned to the room, the thing she had stuffed in a drawer under makeup samples and leaflets. Not a breeze in the room, all quiet. Not even the wide-open window could coax any air to enter.

A scrapbook with magazine clippings, reports from the Tohoku earthquake with stories of the dead and missing. There were pictures, men and women of various ages and little children with solemn eyes, sometimes even an entire family, everyone lost to the great tsunami and no time for any goodbyes. The back of the book had a shot that was taken professionally in a studio, a mom with two girls in kimono, both in their mid-teens and so similar in appearance they could have been twins. One of them was Mutsumi, her hair in a flower ribbon, a shy smile on her oval face.

There were no rules for her room when she wasn't home, just an assumption I wouldn't be stupid and betray her trust. But then, seeing her rush to the desk and shut the drawer as soon as I walked in, I had wondered what might be in there to keep from me at all cost. That afternoon, I surrendered. Five steps and a little peek and I stared at the faded photo, wishing it weren't true. The electrical fan hummed helplessly in a corner as a toy store gained in dimension. Behind pretty faces and dresses that everyone loved, some of the toys had complicated lives and hearts crushed by horrendous events, only the toys had learned not to show this and keep holding their pain deep inside, all the while dragging themselves to work and making copies and pouring tea and never a hair out of place, and then the American shuffled in: "Why so serious?"

Sitting down for another shower, I stared at myself in the

mirror. Alone on an island, no plans and no friends as I waited for a waitress to get off work. No reason to be on the island save for a job where I played a mascot, resigned to mark time while my dreams of professional acting were shrinking in front of my eyes. The years went by and my face didn't speak for the times, while deep down I had started to sense that acting might not be my calling but merely a hope that could end. The thought gave me pause, then despair and fear.

The oldsters were still in the tub when I left, soaking and lost in their thoughts. Perfect candidates for forgetting their towels.

It was some sort of revelation to see Mutsumi in front of her club, bowing farewell to a customer, a gentleman in a suit who seemed more than three sheets to the wind. Behind them, on top of the carpeted stairs, stood a bouncer with gold-rimmed shades who guarded a dark velvet rope, the gate into sexual fantasy.

Mutsumi looked stunning in a long blue dress that shimmered under the neon, yet even more stunning was her demeanor. As the man clambered into a cab, one doddering move at a time, she fussed over his coat with deference while avoiding his drunken paws, her voice like a mother indulging a child. I didn't know her, I realized. The strain that her work required and what the Japanese call "day and night faces," the pride that she had to swallow to pay for the life she had chosen. All the more shocking to see her anger as she waved the cab out of sight.

"Adieu, *mon chère*." Her eyes were a tragic new wave. "May your wife have the guts to divorce you."

As we walked down Kagurazaka-dori, her shoulders hunched with disdain, I understood why she wasn't listening or why she would feel that she didn't owe anything to a man anywhere in the world.

"A rough day at work?"

"My new boss. Of all the assholes in Tokyo, that guy takes the cake."

"Is there . . . harassment?"

She shook her head. "A guest said that I looked tired, that I wasn't paying attention. He told my boss and that started drama, and now I'm sure I can't sleep tonight."

"A movie might help. *Destroy All Monsters* is next."

"I'm sick of monsters and watching TV. It doesn't solve anything."

She kicked off her heels in the hallway, sending them into a corner as if renouncing the ways of the world. Four in the morning and she tackled the fridge, brooding and full of loathing, hauling snacks to her room where the door slammed like an exclamation point.

The sheets thrown off and the fan humming by my side, I heard her slippers shuffle to the bathroom, too many drinks at the club. She blew her nose, an act of despair, then sniffled like a little child. In her room, the dressers flung open as if she were leaving on the next ship. A sigh of despair, then the television—the last line of defense against dreams that were ready to pounce. Soon I realized what she was watching. A shriek and a whoosh of atomic breath, a creature stomping on powerlines, cornered and nowhere to go and the enemies closing in.

Destroy All Monsters in a private screening, the ultimate pits of unhappiness.

It was shared with me, one night in our kitchen, that Gaston was born in Algeria and had immigrated to France at age five, first settling in Nantes and Marseilles and now planning to move to Paris. A Japanophile and an advocate of immigrant rights, he owned a used bookstore down on the Left Bank, which Mutsumi pronounced in French with a sense of consummate awe. In her telling, he was a mix between a handsome intellectual and a thought leader in the Middle East, the one man she could ever respect. I never knew her to be political, yet she was yearning to be a serious person, to evolve from watching Godzilla and start on the Battle of Algiers.

"What if he lied to get you to Paris? What if you end up lost and abandoned?"

"My god—you are jealous!"

"You know I don't hate you. It's not a secret."

I stood at the stove making *oyakodon*, a rice bowl with chicken and egg. The electrical fans hummed away, the air limp from the heat of the day. Mutsumi almost never cooked but had ample advice for me, from the way that the rice should simmer to the exact amount of soy sauce needed. All of a sudden, her face grew quiet.

Having grown up without a family, she knew there were things that she hadn't learned, an awareness of self only others could help her obtain. She knew that some people considered her strange and that this made her life more difficult, she just didn't know how to change it. Attractive and smart as she was, she fell through the cracks on an island of rules and tradition, a mindset apart from the herd.

"What else should I know?" She came closer, all shampoo and dancer legs. "I know you like me, the way you keep staring."

"I like how you live. How you make your own choices."

It was now or never, the moment of truth. She gave me a short, strange look, and for the first time in all the weeks we had shared a small humid apartment, we were drawn to the same thing in each other. The finish line, roommates be damned. After seconds of awkward maneuvering, my mouth found hers and we closed our eyes.

"Is it son of Godzilla?"

Mutsumi smiled at the tent in my pants. Her hands linked in the back of my neck that was damp in the humid kitchen, and Gaston might have strangled me with a scarf had he seen the smile on my face. Her cheekbone was close to mine as she stroked my hair gently, exploring the unknown feel. All of a sudden, her body stiffened.

"I'm so sorry . . ." She drew away, a kingdom betrayed. I stood still as though having been slapped.

"Are you kidding? Is this some sort of twisted experiment?"

"It's not that simple . . ."

"No problem, I'll make it simple. You're either interested or you're not—and if not, then let's stop dangling carrots. I'm not one of your stupid customers."

My turn to rush off and slam doors—voilà, the elan! I stormed out of the house and into the street with a boner that wanted to break things. A woman, of course, may change her mind at all times. And then a man may hate her for that.

The night ended at a diner, smooth jazz and all empty seats, where a barman with small, sad eyes became my last friend on earth. He listened silently to my rants like a solo trombone in the jazz, shooting glances at my empty glass and refilling all the way to dawn. I was mad at Mutsumi and the whole damn city, sad and beautiful Tokyo that didn't need me and had spurned me like everyone else. Most of all, I was mad at myself, the way my life had become a French romance. *Tell me you're happy, Eloise, and if not, whatever the reason, let's find a small little thing for diversion, any small silly thing at all, to start filling this nasty emptiness when they keep saying the world should be ours.*

"You okay?" the barman asked me at closing. I could barely stand or make sense.

"All good, man. I love your tie."

"It's not my business . . ." he said carefully. "I think she likes you. She said no so she wouldn't lose you."

I stumbled along the sidewalk, eyes squinting in the morning sun, then down blue and abandoned streets back to the small apartment. Her door was open, the window as well, the place empty as a monster suit after shooting has wrapped for the day. I rushed out again and kept going, determined to have a talk.

As soon as I entered Club Asia and its ambience of sordid discretion, I saw why Mutsumi was having bad dreams. A large table with fading orchids formed a screen just behind the entrance, making you think of things past their prime. Contoured in the dark were statues of Rubenesque women, which didn't exactly put you in mind of Asia and should have offended Mutsumi. Dotted between statues and orchids on high-legged stools were the tables, small white ovals that seated facelessly talking men beside women whose eyes counted minutes.

It was long past the time to close, two days after our scene in the kitchen, when I came in to look for Mutsumi. I saw her at one of the tables, next to a man who looked like a toad inexplicably dressed in a suit. He was eating a piece of tart with a miniscule silver spoon, and from his measured, unhurried manner, the way his fingers were gripping the spoon and the cake moved around in his mouth, you not only knew that he owned the club but that he thought the staff were his, too.

Mutsumi motioned me over and told me she couldn't leave. A customer from out of town, she wasn't sure when she would be home. Her makeup was smeared from what might have been tears.

"What is this?" Blood rushed behind my temples. "You don't have to stay if you don't want to."

The toad put the spoon on the plate, a move of controlled impatience. "Get lost, kiddo," he murmured softly. "Before there is needless hurt."

I wasn't ready for what came next, a moment of nasty multitudes. Mutsumi rose with a comment that even toads consider offensive, then the toad grabbed her small behind and shoved her back in the seat. My arm snapped back on an impulse, the hand in a fist, but I had rammed a waiter behind me and sent a tray with champagne flutes smashing into quiet orchids. The rest was mean, a grunting of men at work. The bouncer rushed in from outside and flanked moodily over the plants, then a deep existential sadness washed over me as my ear turned hot from a punch. A line from a Godzilla movie flashed through my terrified mind: *The shrill sound is not a malfunction. We have lost control of the monsters.* The rest was yelling and heavy breathing, an aimless melee of swings that had me stumble and land in the curtains, some punches well thrown, others not, then glass on the floor and blood in my face and overall plenty of needless hurt.

Mutsumi came home that night, beating me by a week. The cops took their own sweet time and appeared to take genuine interest in the nature of our roommate arrangement. A hostess and a foreign actor? Do explain! By the time I had signed an apology to the club and could leave the detention center, five stitches on a humbled jaw, a crown missing in my teeth, Mutsumi had left for Paris. Her stuff was gone save for dresses, some shoes she had worn at the club. Her smell lingered in the apartment, a trace of her rose perfume, and despite ample airing for days I thought it was still around when the letter arrived in the mail. A neat feminine hand, the words all carefully drawn.

Dearest Lee,

I'm so sorry for all that happened, and so sorry not to say goodbye. I had to move up my departure as the club was just being impossible. I hope you've fully recovered and are enjoying the apartment, the quiet without me. A new tenant should be there next month, but feel free to take my old room.

Paris is wonderful—a new life. I've found work as a waitress and will soon move in with Gaston. A roof apartment in Montparnasse, can you believe it? There's a patisserie downstairs and the almond croissants are just like Chez Jacques.

I miss you and Kagurazaka. I cannot say this well, but it helped me that you were there. I was going through something strange and without you, I'm not sure what might have happened. I'll never again see Godzilla without thinking of us in my room. A bit addicted perhaps, weren't we?

Sometimes memories make us sad, but then, sometimes they also help. I've locked this summer away in a box and put the box away on a shelf. It is there for me always, to think of my last months in Tokyo.

Thank you so much for your kindness. Should you ever make it to Paris, please do say hello.

Always yours, and à bientôt,

—M

I never made sense of Mutsumi, the things she said in that letter. I thought that her move was misguided, that she was running away from herself and just taking her hang-ups to Paris for the unwitting French to deal with. Another escape, like the monster movies, as if changing countries could solve any problems.

Too proud at the time to admit that I missed her, and too full of myself to see the genuine affection in her letter, I ended up ghosting Mutsumi. Never came out to visit Paris, never answered her letter or the postcard the following month, stamped La Chapelle, not Montparnasse. I made fun of the box with memories, telling myself that Godzilla was ruined as were French things of any kind.

Not that it matters—we're not likely to meet again, both of us moving so much—but there are doubts in my mind that the rooftop apartment existed. Or for that matter, a man named Gaston. I cannot picture Mutsumi in love, waking up next to a man and asking what he wants for breakfast. I can see her in Paris, however, a tall Asian in a belted coat enjoying art galleries and museums and roaming boulevards free as a bird, then sitting down in a small café and starting a conversation with art lovers who have joined her, smitten with her accented French. The thought shouldn't make me jealous or sad, because nothing had happened between us.

Autumn arrived in Kagurazaka, a new chill in the morning air as I rolled my suitcase down to the station. A few acorns rolled past, like in a Japanese nursery song. I had lost my spot on the show and was headed for beautiful Seoul, where my agent had said I was needed to play an alien in a smartphone commercial. They liked my work and my large blue eyes, he said, and the fact they could get me cheap. As of next week, two Japanese students would share the apartment, which was close to their university.

"Where's the girl? The one with the pretty eyes?"

The waiter at Chez Jacques was setting up chairs, looking curiously at my face.

I regarded the place one more time, the wooden tables outside, the round tree with yellow leaves, and I sensed what I would feel after leaving. The summer in the apartment—the nights in her room, the fan humming ineffectively, the scent from her unmade bed. What had we been throughout all this time? More than roommates and something like friends, sharing a summer, then going our separate ways. Sometimes you meet someone at a certain time and that person hits close to your heart, they touch you in a certain way, a way that is crucial for your life at exactly that moment in time. They may challenge you, make you remember or think about things in a way that you hadn't before. You may not change moving on through life, but the person and moment in time, they remain in your mind forever. A knock on your door: "Are you up? Wanna watch something?" A woman in her pajamas, an old poster on a bathroom door.

L'amour c'est être stupide ensemble. To be in love is to be stupid together.

Good luck to you both, Gaston and Mutsumi.

A Spy in the House of Manju

THE LIGHTS WERE already out at the desk when Ame rang the small muffled bell, struck by how loud it seemed in the silence. A door banged somewhere inside, and from behind an old *noren* curtain emerged the receptionist. A skinny man in his thirties, dressed in a uniform suit, his hair mussed in a wavy part. Without apology or seeming to notice her, he made a note in the daybook register, then his eyes took her in at last.

"Welcome to the Manju Muramatsu. Your name and duration of stay?"

"Two nights, Matsubara. Attending a funeral, the old janitor here."

"Ah, the funeral. A friend of the family?"

"The granddaughter. I live in America."

The receptionist looked up, perplexed, then took a step back and fussed with his pens. A look at the passport, then at Ame, then again at her place of birth, as if somehow insistent checking could make the data align. An uneasy riddle, she existed in between meanings.

"You mean, you are Japanese?"

"It's all in there." Ame glanced at the passport.

"Of course, yes indeed. And you work . . . in America?"

"I'm in sales, at a bookstore."

"A bookstore, I see. In America. Oh—please do not lean on the counter. The wood is all Japanese. A bit brittle."

For a lot of Japanese people, nothing is harder to absorb and accept as fact, nothing rattles their faith in the norms of reality more profoundly, than a person who looks Japanese, has a Japanese passport and name, and then opens her mouth and speaks broken Japanese. A breakdown of meaning and association, like jelly coming out of a faucet. The question of what she was now stumped the receptionist the way it had stumped the officer at the airport, the customs man who asked her questions while his schnauzer had sniffed at her pants, then sneezed with mild disapproval. Having taken out her shirts and underwear and probed every inch of the suitcase which he was certain carried drugs from America, apologizing for the delay while clearly thinking about removing the lining, the officer had waved her through, and then there was Japan.

"This place seems old. In a good way, I mean."

"Indeed, it is period charm. We have been here since early Meiji, the first Western-style hotel in Japan."

The receptionist used simplified Japanese, pointing down on the floorboards as he mentioned the word Japan.

"The Muramatsu family has its own manju recipe, so they call us the House of Manju. You can get some in our shop as a souvenir. I mean, if Japanese sweets are your taste."

The history of the place was palpable, so solemn that it hushed the voice and made you wonder about the past. A sense of heaviness emanated from the hallways, the old photographs on oak-paneled walls showing guests and some of the staff. Among yellowed newspaper articles, Ame recognized Helen Keller and a Hungarian magician in the 1930s, enjoying a manju pastry as the world outside went to hell.

Ame was beat from the flight and the train ride out to Hakone, a resort town famous for hot springs, ninety minutes southwest of

Tokyo. A bus at the station had taken her through misted mountain roads, an unmarked stop with a bench. The hotel looked surreal with its blend of traditional Japanese and Victorian-American flourishes, a cluster of eaves and gables, a couple of lighted windows, surrounded by mountains in dreamlike isolation. A massive pagoda roof swept over two floors and the wooden entrance, leaving the chill of a permanent shade. After years of living in Tokyo, how had her grandfather ended up here?

The receptionist took a key from the rack, a motion to follow him. The carpet was faded and smelled faintly like mold, making Ame think of the inns you see in horror movies from South Korea. Half expecting to see a shape charging them with a kitchen knife, she followed the man round a corner, then past a dim archway tucked away in an alcove.

"Never mind this here." The receptionist dismissed the curtain as though he didn't know how it got there. "This bath is . . . a little strange. The old owner had the idea."

Ame slowed her step as she glanced at the curtained archway, but the receptionist kept marching on. When they arrived at her room, he went over the rules of the house, then handed her a set with two keys.

"Breakfast at seven, Western and Japanese-style." He winked in a show of understanding. "If you need something later, please ask for Nomura. That is me."

She was about to enter the room when Nomura turned round in the hallway, awkwardly clearing his throat.

"The deceased is laid out downstairs. The cold room, next to the kitchen. In case you would like to see him."

"He is here?" Her suitcase dropped with a thud.

"It's all arranged. The priest will come in the morning and we'll move him to the crematorium, then take the ashes down to the temple. A nice final resting place." A pause, then he nodded to himself. "The morgue is quite far indeed. I guess it seemed rather a hassle."

Ame had no response. Too much, just too much, the whole damn family.

"Feel free to go and pay your respects," said Nomura. "Just be sure to bring a warm jacket."

The store was empty when Hana called, the books adream on their shelves. Ame came through the rear as always, then turned on the lights at the register and wound up the shutters inside. The building was cold every summer, the heater frequently out of order. Outside, the fog came in from the ocean, searching the alleyways of Japantown like a detective of Nisei dreams.

"I have sad news . . ." her mother began. Her voice sounded muffled, not sure what to do with the sadness.

Nobody knew when exactly her grandfather passed. His condition hadn't been acute, even at ninety-two, according to the nurse on duty. He had slipped away without notice, alone in a hospital room, after a fall in his kitchen at home. No emergency room, no supervision, the doctors caught by surprise. How soon could she come for the funeral?

Ojii-chan had been widowed, estranged from her mother and uncle who had started new lives in America. The vastness of the Pacific, they said, was about the right distance between them. An ocean comes in very handy when you need reasons to miss reunions, when you aim to lose touch with a father who never knew what to do with his children. No interaction and confrontations, no staid lunches in family restaurants on the numerous national holidays. Most news from Tokyo was relayed by Aunt Fumiko, every time when a waitress called her after escorting ojii-chan to his house, too smashed to get home on his own. The children were so embarrassed that Fumiko kept intervening and telling him to behave, but then ojii-chan never changed.

"Say hello to Fumiko and the kids," Hana said. "My apologies we can't be there. Work is crazy and I can't take time off."

A lie smooth as silk. Because practice makes perfect.

The moment you hear that a loved one has died, a conversation becomes instantly useless. As if someone dumped a sack of cement in your lap and said, "Here, hold this," forever, no reason why. You know all that there is to know but have no tools to react or respond. It seems cold to discuss the next steps, the arrangements for the funeral and guests, and whatever else you might say seems frivolous compared to the thing you have heard. More than anything perhaps, you are waiting to get off the phone, to say goodbye and then end the call and start being alone with the news.

Ame stared at the ground, hoping there wouldn't be questions. Her mother knew nothing about her job or the fact that she left the band, and Ame didn't need her opinions on the shiftlessness in her thirties. After all, had it not been Hana first tossing a grenade—moving her family overseas, no matter what others said—into a conservative Japanese family?

The next call came immediately after, an order for a manga calendar and a Golgo 13 figurine.

"Does the package come with the target rifle?"

"Let me check." Ame wiped off tears in a dream. "I think it should be included."

She caught a standby to Haneda the next day. Aunt Fumiko would meet her in Hakone, ten years since her last proper visit.

"You'll see how the place has changed," Hana said before hanging up. "But then, of course, it is still the same."

The room was dark when she opened her eyes, save for the moonlight falling on the ceiling. Two in the morning, the building lay still. For a short, awful moment, she thought there was someone at the door, a ghost in the hallway shuffling her feet. Ame pulled up the blanket closer, her senses now in the room. Around her were smells and things that called up the old familiarity, the echoing footsteps of childhood. Beside the futon was her suitcase on the floor, the luggage tags shimmering in the moonlight. SFO to Haneda, economy. Traveling alone.

Ojii-chan hated Haneda because he hated saying goodbye, the one thing that he came there to do. The day that his wife had left him—the same day, and not accidentally, when he entered retirement and she dreaded him sitting at home, no plans and no clue how to talk to his wife, who he thought would become his maid—had made him the saddest of creatures: the old Japanese man on his own. For a while after that, Ame would come over New Year's and spend a week at his house.

Ironically, they had asked her, the other lost sheep in the family, to keep him company and off the sauce. She was to check if he wasted money or gave gifts to the pretty waitress at the Chinese restaurant down the street. Like she was some sort of foreign spy. In fact, Ame had no objection if her grandfather blew his pension, especially on a waitress making minimum wage. He had cheated death long ago, then was spoiled for years by expense accounts, so now he maintained the largesse. What else to do at this point with his money? His three children, two of them in America and working for minimum wage, had refused his support with a vengeance.

Mostly they sat in the tatami room, slouched on cushions in front of the TV and munching the fruit sandwiches that he loved, until ojii-chan fell asleep and Ame covered him with a blanket, then turned off the lights and the television. Every time she got up for the bathroom, he would rise and remind her sleepily to be careful not to tear the *shoji*, the sliding doors with the paper screens. Until they got torn, that is. Super thin, the old shoji.

They had no tools to talk to each other, to understand a life that was different. Ojii-chan never left the island, not in all of his ninety years, not even for a weekend in Seoul, then he died close to where he was born. Odd for a former pilot, he had said he was scared of flying and dying in a plane crash, helpless. He never knew what it meant to be different or adapt to a foreign environment, the desperate need to fit in. He couldn't imagine what it was like to be the sole Japanese in a high school in San Mateo, sitting in history class with growing unease as the 1930s approached. The Great Depression and Steinbeck novels; the Japanese in Manchuria, the massacres at Nanjing.

Every time they had a new textbook, Ame checked how that time was covered, the illustrations and quotes they had. She would count the pages until the war, the attack on Pearl Harbor, hoping they would run out of time or the teacher might focus on Rosie the Riveter. Pearl Harbor was bad, but Nanjing was the absolute pits. The kids in the class were interested in a massacre and kept asking the teacher questions about bayoneted women and children, stealing glances at the Asian in the room. Ame fixed her eyes on the book without seeing any of the text, her face burning hot as she wished she could disappear. They seemed to think that her grandfather was a monster, a man who raped and killed Chinese girls in a frenzy of racial hate.

Ame herself didn't know her grandfather, didn't know what there was to know. She never disliked or feared him the way her mother and Shunsuke did. As their eyes met, they both knew that it wasn't possible to know how the other lived. They respected that about each other, sitting and watching TV until ojii-chan started snoring. She never mentioned the sirens, the ambulances in the night, that made him start up from sleep and mumble they must run for shelter, run from the bombs, take the children.

Seeing her off at the airport, he would read his conservative newspaper while she walked around getting snacks, then sit with her in the lounge as the time for goodbyes ran out. They never spoke till her flight was called, never hugged as they rose with a sigh. They weren't putting on a brave face, they just didn't know how to act until at last they could wave goodbye and she passed through the massive gate, the portal to her other life. It didn't seem strange, not to them. Some people say they are bad at goodbyes, but perhaps what they mean is they hate separation, the letting go that tears at your heart. Ame and ojii-chan weren't like that; they were bad at the actual goodbye. Nothing equipped them for the moment either, and they knew and respected that too.

Ame had sometimes wondered if her grandfather sat there a little longer, perhaps smoking one of his cigars and leafing through *Sankei Shimbun* as he had done for some sixty years, before shuffling back to the monorail, the interminable ride back home on the elevated tracks to Hamamatsu, then a bus back to the small apartment, his life by himself where the days were uneventfully similar and he closed the paper screens carefully. She never had a chance to ask because one year, he suddenly canceled. A hospital stay for an operation put an end to the yearly visits.

"A bus to America . . ." he mumbled one day in the lounge, his eyes on the board for departures.

"What did you say?"

"If there was a bus, I could visit. See how your mother is doing." Ojii-chan sighed, then remembered as though in a dream.

"When you were small, just a little girl, I had a map of the world in my house. You spent hours looking at places, imagining what they were like. One day, when your mom still came over, you saw America on the map and asked how to take the bus there. You were curious about America, even then."

Ame sat up in bed, checking the clock on the nightstand. Nothing stirred in the room or the hallway, the building was quiet as the ages. Still disoriented from the travel, she knew she wouldn't get any more sleep. Not bothering with the old floor lamp, she got out of bed and shuffled over to the window, the floor creaking ominously under her feet.

Behind her own face reflected, the moon in Hakone looked beautiful. The pine trees and mountains were still in the dark, but the grass in the back of the building was showing the first gray of dawn. Nothing moved in the dreamlike isolation.

Why did I have to go when no one else would? Why am I the weird messenger girl?

Two floors down, her grandfather lay in the cold room. Waiting for his own funeral, the last rite for him on earth. He had believed that funerals were nonsense, a waste of cash thrown at priests in exchange for an afterlife promise. That Japanese people fear them because, as the priest taps a drum and chants the unending sutras, you must sit on the floor, legs bent, your buns on your heels, which is such agony on the knees that through the whole length of the rite, you aren't able to have a straight thought, let alone remember the dead. When they allow you to get up at last, legs feeble like a drunken sailor and tears in your blinking eyes, you feel less overcome with the grief than relieved from the maddening pain. It is funny, the wobbling legs, but a funeral must be somber and serious to where no one shall see you wobble. Or at least that was how he told it.

The fact that he lived in the past didn't keep him from hating sentimentality, unless it was tied to the war. He teared up when he watched the old movies, the scenes where a young kamikaze says goodbye to his family and heads out in a rickety plane toward certain death on the sea. Some planes had cherry blossoms painted on the side, a symbol of beautiful short-livedness.

Ame knew she had to go down and tell him the final goodbye, then relay the message from Mom, perhaps even hold a short wake. It was the reason why she was here, why she came all the way to Japan, the mists of Hakone. Only how did you say goodbye to an old man you never knew?

None of the authors who had stayed at the hotel were familiar to Ame, although famous novels were penned there. On a deadline and hounded by editors to submit, authors came there in need of quiet, registering under an alias and holing up in a room until their work was completed. Meals and tea were provided by the hotel, as well as paper and sharpened pencils and a small statue of the patron saint of deadlines, who would watch over sleepless nights as a reminder of promises made. Months might pass until a writer emerged from his room, having mailed the manuscript to a publisher.

One night in the 1950s, a tragedy struck. A young poetess, the author of feminist haiku, hanged herself in the flower palace suite. She wasn't famous, perhaps not even working on poems, but her death had made waves for a while and her last book sold rather well. Ame couldn't imagine earning money that way, sitting in a room all day and writing down things in your head until you whip something into a shape that people pay money to read and enjoy. No wonder, she thought, so many writers committed suicide. According to one of the articles, the bellhop who found the poetess had given notice the following day, afraid that her ghost was haunting the halls.

Ame stood in a hallway, hunched in the morning chill as she studied the articles on the wall. Her mind centered on an idle question, something none of the news had mentioned. What room did she hang herself in? Had they renamed the flower palace suite?

When Aunt Fumiko had phoned in the morning, she took the call from a booth in the lobby. "You can stay with us if you like, come see the new house. The kids would be happy to see you."

"I'm leaving tomorrow. Awfully short, but work gave me only two days."

The same excuse her mother had used. Smooth as silk, because practice makes perfect. Because ghosting family makes awkward funerals.

"No time to see your father? Maybe stop by in Hiroshima?"

"He doesn't know I am here. We thought it better, just simpler." Ame's voice almost caught in her throat.

The family laws in Japan didn't recognize joint custody at the time. Like other divorcées there, her parents opted to make a clean break where her father wouldn't see the child or be involved in her life anymore. The arrangement was based on love, they said, sparing their daughter the sadness, the pain of a million goodbyes as she shuttled between two parents who couldn't acknowledge each other. Hana liked to keep her life simple and her sins away from the child, and now surely wasn't the time to attempt a reunion in Hiroshima.

Lucky me, Ame thought, to be loved like that.

"I was shocked they would put him in a cold room," she said. "Is that even legal?"

"There wasn't much choice. And finances being what they are..." Aunt Fumiko sighed. "Let's meet in the lobby at ten. You'll need a kimono, some prayer beads—it's just us there at the cremation. Perhaps the waitress from the Chinese restaurant, but I told her to stay away. To think how much he has left her . . ."

Ame skipped the regular breakfast and headed instead for the bakery, curious about the *mizu manju*. One of the articles on the wall explained that the hotel once had cows on the grounds and they even produced their own margarine, a staple at Japanese hotels that symbolized foreign culture, the good life enjoyed by those in the West.

The staff was confused by her Japanese, then asked if she needed chopsticks. Ame was mildly upset—who the hell uses chopsticks for a sweet bun?—but when she tried the first bite, the dough was exactly right, soft and translucent, almost like jelly, warm in her mouth like an autumn Sunday. The mizu manju tasted like childhood, the smells of a morning bakery.

Back in the room, she sat down on the freshly made bed, trying to map out her sightseeing. The town of Hakone had a picturesque river and a shopping street lined with food stalls. There was Mount Fuji and Lake Ashinoko shrouded in cold ancient mist, and next to the tree-lined shore, the vacation home of the emperor. The place looked nice and she began making all sorts of plans, when the jet lag hit her like bricks. She sank onto the bed, limbs weak, her whole being aching to sleep and forcing her eyes to close. Then it was curtains, a dark embrace.

Born in 1926, at the end of the short Taisho era, Hideo Matsubara had outlived his certain death, a lonely death in a small plane above the ocean, by well over seven decades. The day that he turned eighteen, he received the dreaded red paper, the draft from the Imperial Army that was then still delivered in person. He was called for immediate duty with the Divine Wind Special Attack Unit, known in the West as the kamikaze. He had dreamed of becoming a pilot, but the times were of war and, tragically, some missions had pilots sent out to sea and never return from there. Like birds in the skies of a hopeless battle, they were supposed to die honorable deaths by slamming their planes into battleships, the Americans approaching Japan.

Matsubara was ready to be sacrificed for the nation, a blossom thrown to the winds. It was the order and expectation, and he was too young to fully imagine that death was something forever. He had no beef with the Chinese or Americans, never grasped what had started the war or why he was fighting for prosperity in Asia, and it was only through luck of the draw that he managed to stay alive. By the time his number was up, they had run out of flying machines to send away into battle. The young pilot was relieved, then disappointed, having missed his one stab at glory.

Perhaps out of survivor guilt, he spoke with disdain of the kamikaze who returned from the mission, those stalled by equipment failure or worse, a failing of nerves. By the end of the war, most planes that Japan had left were garbage heaps with wings attached, any loosely wired piece of junk that might somehow manage a takeoff. Some pilots trained on the ground, using small wooden tubs on wheels to learn how to fly a real plane, a training some wouldn't survive. No wonder some had second thoughts as they penned their poem of death. One pilot returned three times when he was shot on the spot by an officer, who no longer felt that this kamikaze was the right stuff for an attack. Ame felt terrible when she heard the story. She would have done the same thing, she thought, coming back with a lame excuse as to why again, sincerest apologies, she was foiled in her duty for the emperor.

The kamikaze was the only time when Matsubara discussed his past. He might mention the insurance company, an assistant with lovely dresses, a boss who would shout himself hoarse, but the stories would always fade as if the details no longer mattered. The company was his life, he said, the one place since the end of the war that had given him a sense of belonging, a meaning he never found at home with his wife and children. And so Ame had been surprised when, after retirement, he had worked again as a janitor.

"It wasn't a job, not exactly. Your grandfather was mostly retired."

Nomura served a cup of hot sake with a small economical flourish. He was staffing the bar at night, a dark space of cavernous pine where Ame warmed up with sake and soup that Nomura had fixed in the kitchen. Enveloped by mist from the mountains, the hotel seemed stuck in a permanent chill.

"He called a plumber once in a while, telling them what to fix. Then eventually, he retired from that. He didn't need much, as long as he wasn't a burden."

"Has anyone come to see him?"

"Your grandfather was . . . rather private." Nomura looked down at his hands. "It is normal at his age, I suppose. His friends were all former colleagues, and eventually he cut them off. Took himself off alumni lists, no more cards at the end of the year. He didn't like to be around old people, he once said. Only talked to the pretty waitress."

"I didn't know that." Ame was shocked.

"He turned eighty and we thought about arrangements, a space in the temple for when the time came. Then when he turned ninety and things being busy, we sort of forgot. Like, we forgot he could actually pass, like he himself didn't know how to die. Then last week, we remembered."

The cold had awoken Ame, her stomach rumbling as she took a shower. Never mind about seeing sights, it was time to find the hotel bar, where Nomura doubled as barman still wearing the same suit and tie. The barroom was empty save for an old man sunk in an armchair, snoring away in a dream. A jazz standard came from the speakers as Nomura was closing the register, then started to dry the dishes.

"Where is everybody?" said Ame. "Isn't it summer season?"

"The weekends pick up, couples coming from Tokyo. Little getaways, that sort of thing." His tone suggested the extramarital.

"No more writers holed up in their rooms?"

"Pardon me?"

Nomura stopped wiping a glass. "That is long ago, we haven't had writers in years. Anyway, we enjoy the quiet." He put down the glass, then lowered his voice confidentially.

"Some people, you see, they say this place is a little strange. Like something out of Edogawa Rampo." He paused, then added, "I'm sorry. Of course, you don't know Edogawa Rampo."

"We have his books in the store. Some Americans read him."

"In America . . ." Nomura started but paused, mired in sudden complexity. Nodding thoughtfully to himself, he put the glass away on a shelf and then folded the towel with care, draping it on a rack. By the time everything was in its place, his question had been abandoned.

Ame regarded Nomura with a sense of envy. He was grounded in his surroundings, the facts of his life, as instantly recognizable as the thing that he was and represented as a tree in its native soil. No need for him to explain and answer all sorts of questions for others to understand. It was different for her, much more work, a stray limb on the family tree.

"Almost ten." Nomura put down the towel. "The downstairs must be locked for the night. Should go soon if you want to see him."

His voice held a mild reproof, as though he were asking politely what the hell kind of family was this. Ame realized she was anxious, her hands slightly shaking. Memories came of sitting with ojii-chan at Haneda, two people in an airport lounge, not wanting to linger and not knowing how to say goodbye, so much unsaid and time running out. She should pay her respects now, tell her grandfather about her life or some version that sounded nice, the same version she told her mother and maybe herself. But she kept stalling, waiting for as long as possible, checking the clock on the wall that ticked time with a sense of foreboding. Aunt Fumiko was right, the whole thing was strange, so strange it was almost scary.

Ame downed the rest of the sake, then rose shakily and thanked Nomura. It is true, she thought, they make stronger drinks in the countryside. All the way to the end of the barroom, the wide wooden doors and then down the stairs, her legs were all wobbly and weak like a real Japanese at a funeral.

The opening door brought the cold, along with the smell of meat and the incense in bowls on the shelves. Ame bowed quickly and stepped into the dimness, resolved that she wouldn't stay long, just enough to say she had been there.

He was laid out on woolen blankets, his hairless head on a cushion. Under the shoulders and lower back, the pity of his shrunken body, they had put plastic packs with dry ice. Ame looked at the pale, solemn face, the cotton stuffed in the nose, the cheeks that had hollowed with age. He would be like this until the cremation, when his remnants of bones and ashes would fill a ceramic urn.

It was strange to see ojii-chan in a kimono, not the sweatpants and shirts he wore at the house. The kimono was crossed in front, the right side over the left, the heart that no longer moved. Placed near one hand was a pack of cigars, a thing for him to hold on to as he was crossing the great divide.

Ame thought of the seven decades her grandfather had cheated from death. Seven decades to go to work and drink beer and eat ramen at Chinese restaurants, to get married and father three children, then see his wife leave and two children escape from Japan. As she looked at the lifeless face that held no more power to make anyone feel embarrassed, Ame wished that her mother was there. Seeing her grandfather like this, the way he was handled by strangers and lying there all by himself, made her angry at the whole family. Too absorbed in their lives and too scared to connect, they couldn't even do right by the dead.

She leaned over the face in the casket, so solemn, alone with itself. Tears left her eyes, warm and soft.

"Thank you for everything. I'm so sorry no one could be here."

The memories that take courage, the thing Hana wasn't able to do. Always hiding behind the ocean, the time zones and too much work, always asking to send her messages. Once the hiding goes on for a while, it is hard to go back and connect, to see all the years you have missed. Hana was free now that ojii-chan died, released from the shadow he cast, but in that freedom, there was a new sadness.

Ame wanted to stay, just a little longer, but the room was getting awfully cold. With tears on her cheeks, she took the fruit sandwich from the airport and placed it inside the casket, next to the feet in the white tabi socks. A random thought came, a memory back from high school when her date was a no-show and she came home and told Hana the boy must have gotten cold feet, and then Hana, still learning English, had gasped, "Oh my god, he is dead?"

"We are thinking of you . . ." she whispered, relaying the message from Hana. "Everybody is doing well. You can see us watching from above."

She bowed twice in front of the casket, then turned and slipped out of the room. The door closed on a helpless silence. A plane on a morning tarmac, an old pilot coming home at last.

They were bad at the leaving, the goodbyes in an airport lounge. They respected that about each other, always would. Until they could meet again, little blossoms in the afterworld.

The curtain in the alcove opened up to a changing room, wooden lockers and benches and a dust-coated scale. Behind that was a small, tiled chamber that was lit by a single bulb. According to a sign, the bath was fed from a spring in the mountains, which meant that the thick green color of the water was actually pure and rejuvenating. The touch of earthiness was completed by a smell of sulfur, dark stones lining the bath in a mosaic.

After putting her clothes in a locker and entering the dim chamber, Ame saw why Nomura had said that the onsen was a little strange. A massive ceramic phallus, faded and chipped in a shade of pale green, towered over the steaming water. A little help to get guests in the mood, the least subtle hint in all of Japan. Sweet Jesus, thought Ame, not in my bath.

She eased herself into the water, as far away from the thing as possible. The tiles had a lovely pattern and the temperature was just right, and a warm laziness relaxed her. The alcohol in her system made her feel a little bit dizzy, but there was a homey feeling watching the steam on the stones. Without the ceramic, she thought, this onsen really was perfect.

The woman didn't announce herself, just slid the door open and stepped through the curtain, then slipped off her shoes in the changing room. Undressing in the light of a lamp, she had an uncanny resemblance to Ame. Again, she thought of the movies where someone meets their own double at an inn and gets stabbed with a kitchen knife, but then as the woman let down her hair, shoulder-length and streaked with soft gray, Ame saw that she wasn't her double.

"I hope you don't mind." The woman moved to the bath, whisper-quiet.

"Lots of space. If you don't mind some degenerate art." Ame glanced at the ceramic phallus.

The woman made no response, just nodded to mean she had seen it. Ame liked how she didn't comment or show any sign of upset. Just like, "Ah, that old thing."

"A quick soak, then back to the grind." She slipped into the tub with a sigh. "I'm on a deadline, one more page and the book is done."

"A writer?"

The woman chuckled. "At least till my publisher gets the manuscript. After that, God knows what I'll be. Perhaps staffing a konbini out in the sticks."

"I didn't know writers still stayed here. Someone said it was a thing of the past."

For a while, they were soaking in silence, a few feet apart, gazing at the old tiles and ignoring the penis. Ame was glad they were both relaxed, that the woman didn't seem to notice she was speaking in strange Japanese. Perhaps back home, she imagined, they could be friends and meet up and talk about life and books. The tattoos really helped in Japan. Most people appeared relieved when they saw the ink on her forearms, because everything now made sense, there was a label they understood. An alien from another planet; all bets are off and no expectations.

"Are you here for the funeral?" the woman asked conversationally. "I heard the old janitor passed away."

"Matsubara-san was my grandpa. My mom and I live in America." Ame paused, then the silence encouraged her to continue. "We moved there when I was twelve. My mom wanted to start a new life, away from Japan. I guess I wasn't really consulted."

The woman studied her feet, wrinkled and pink in the heat, as though it might help her think.

"I once wrote a poem about America," she said. "A fridge in a kitchen, humming all night. So noisy because of the size, like stations in outer space. You don't know until you see America that a fridge can make so much noise."

Ame liked the theme of the poem and indeed, American fridges are the noisiest in the world. She had warmed to the woman, her approachable, easy manner, the way she took things as they came without having to comment or judge, but then, bending forward to reach her own feet, she noticed the smell of sake that wafted along on her breath. Perhaps her flushed face wasn't due to the heat? For a moment, Ame wondered if it was smart to share a bath at the Manju Muramatsu with a woman who was a writer, especially close to midnight.

"You like your grandfather?" the woman asked suddenly. "I

mean, how are you holding up?"

"We're not close—but yes, he is nice." For some reason Ame referred to ojii-chan in the present, the way the woman was doing.

"My grandpa was an accountant. The tough, silent type. He would have liked this here decoration." She nodded at the phallus.

"Not too close yourself, it seems."

"He always worked, and in between meetings he kept chasing skirts. But not a mean drunk, at least. Never asked why I wanted to be a poet. 'Just don't write about me,' he said." She made an odd chuckle. "I guess, I liked him. With your own family, it is hard to tell."

"What sort of poems do you write? Anything feminist, or mostly fridges?"

The woman gave Ame a knowing look, then glanced at the clock in the changing room. It was almost eleven.

"I should go—the deadline is midnight." She raised herself from the tub.

As the woman was toweling off, steam rising from her short, plump frame, Ame peered at her from behind and noticed the lack of backside. In a straight, vertical line, her lower back seemed to shape almost smoothly into her upper legs. Ghost ass, Ame thought as the woman slipped into a yukata, the cotton robe for hotels in Japan.

"Nice to meet you," she said. "And good luck with the publication. May I ask, what is your name?"

"I'm Yosano, the pleasure is mine. Good luck with the funeral and everything else. And safe travels home."

The woman was at the entrance, about to slide the doors open, then she turned one more time. "By the way, I like your tattoos. They're very cool."

"Thank you so much. I'll see you around."

Ame regarded her upper arms, then leaned back in the warm green water. She felt better about herself, the challenges of the next day. Almost ready for the awkward funeral and the meeting with her Japanese aunt, perhaps lunch with her children at the house she had never seen. After leaving for home the same day, the midnight bus back to America, she didn't think that she would return soon.

The onsen went back to the quiet, the poetess gone like a sound only a spy would be able to hear.

Shimoyama and the Absent Ghost

IT WAS THE day before Christmas, the same year as the great earthquake when his wife had vanished in the tsunami, when Shimoyama sat in a taxi on his way to Yamamoto station. He planned to catch an express to Sendai and then the bullet train on to Tokyo, where he would look for a job and a prostitute. At the wheel was his father-in-law, Ando, a solemn man in his seventies who was speeding as if a tsunami were at their heels, turning from time to time to address Shimoyama.

"The seats are shot." He avoided a tree on a curve. "Smells like cigarettes and old men."

Shimoyama looked at the snow that was heaped on the sides of the road. His planning had been meticulous. Arrive in Ueno at six, find the pleasure district near the station and let himself be approached on the stroll, a show of reluctance, then negotiation and deal. A simple enough transaction, occurring hundreds of times every day. And yet, he was apprehensive. Was the pleasure district, run by yakuza mobsters and patrolled by a token police beat, really safe for a schoolteacher from the sticks? Could he trust the woman not to attempt a snatch at his wallet, or worse, shortchange him on the service he desired? He shuddered to think that his scheme might end up a waste.

At the station in Yamamoto, a mannerly spat ensued over the fare. Ando waived it, but Shimoyama knew he needed the cash. Fares had dropped since the great tsunami and Ando avoided the devastated areas, afraid that the fares might be ghosts who asked to return to their homes, the streets that no longer existed. More than anything, Shimoyama wished no more debt, no more favors to repay to Ando after everything he owed already. The shelter and help with the authorities, the old bicycle to get around. The tsunami had claimed his house and every last possession inside, leaving only the clothes on his back and a satchel with grammar quizzes, useless now when there remained ruins where the school building once had stood.

"Best of luck, and write us sometime." Ando steamed breath in the cold.

'I'll be in touch once I've settled in."

"And make sure you add salt to the food there. Tokyo taste is weak for Tohoku people."

Ando treated his son-in-law as though he were Japanese. Shimoyama had adopted their name, as he didn't think of returning to America, not even after what had happened. Of course, the people in the town kept asking when he was planning to move back home, but Shimoyama would look surprised and say he was now Japanese.

Beyond lampposts and snow-covered tracks, in the darkness of pines that stretched all the way down to the sea, a face flickered for an instant. A housedress showed among trees, muddied and stained, then vanished in the dark beyond. Shimoyama attempted to speak but the wind gusted up from the sea, hunching his shoulders and choking the words. Thankfully, the chance was missed.

As they bowed without meeting eyes, the two men displayed no emotion, not betraying in any manner that they assumed the goodbye to be final, that for a long time and for reasons never voiced or questioned and reassessed, they wouldn't see each other again.

The lights came on in the train. The sole passenger in the carriage that smelled of old clothes, Shimoyama took the obento from his suitcase. A lacquer box with rice and salmon, a side dish of tsukemono. Minami liked the salted pickles more than he, and sometimes at the end of the month, when his salary couldn't cover any meats, she had served them with rice and miso soup and teased him to enjoy the staple, the pickles crunching merrily in her mouth.

Every day we ate tsukemono, and now she can never eat it again. But I still sit here and eat tsukemono, can try tsukemono that Minami never knew. I'm still here, not this time, not quite yet.

He felt relief at surviving his wife, and then shame for feeling relieved. Then over time came a sense of mortality that had frightened him to the bone—if Minami could end, so could he—and along with that, new resolve. He knew the tsunami had not distinguished: his outliving others was luck in a horrible drawing of straws. Like an animal shot in the hills, panicked and mean, searching for safety as it pressed on a gushing wound, he was perfectly clear in his mind— not about right and wrong or what other people thought he was doing, but the demands of sheer self-preservation, the steps that he needed to take so as not to go quietly mad. He was scared to go quietly mad; he was burdening others already.

As the world loomed large, Shimoyama grew small. He was all that was left now, and all that seemed left to do now was to eat salmon and get the answers he had wanted for many years. He didn't share the sense of endurance, the mandate of silent suffering that had sickened the people around him. Another suicide the week before, an old woman who lost her husband and, in her note, apologized for the bother. It had filled Shimoyama with defiance, the strange sense of superiority that the living have over the dead.

I am still here, watching baseball and my favorite movies. There is still some time left. I am here, breathing in and out, my feet touch the ground: one, two.

He chewed on the tsukemono with eyes in an inward focus, as if tasting delicious sashimi. Then his eyes returned to the window, the silent expanse of the land, and there in the darkness appeared the dream, unbidden.

An absence of man, any traces of life, shaped into mounds and heaps of the rubble that mocked any earthly purpose. Shimoyama saw clothes in the trees, a boat washed up atop a warehouse—surrealist jetsam one knew not what to do with, as surreal as survival itself. He saw cows roaming winter fields, confused after farmers released them, houses folded like strange origami and trucks moving soil that was senselessly radioactive, sent off to where no children played. If he kept staring into the dark, as the dream compelled him to do, he imagined he saw Minami among faces of former students, some his favorites, some a pest who napped openly through his language class, now so many of them rendered ghosts hailing taxis to the devastated areas.

What is it like to die in a tsunami, to be swept out into the sea? And then what do you see after that?

He felt warmed, her deep eyes turned onto his.

"I'm sorry, Samu-chan. I cannot tell you."

"I just wondered . . ."

"It is different from what we imagine, completely different."

"Are there other people? Anyone that we know?"

Her silent eyes told him no.

"Samu-chan, do you miss me?"

"Why, of course."

"I cannot see you sometimes. It is strange, but I can't." She felt for his hand, her touch like a breeze in a tree without leaves.

"Your hand is cold. Are you lonely?"

His hand drew away as the train kept swaying. The wheels clattered softly as they crossed a series of switches, his destination approaching.

"Tokyo must be exciting. Isn't it what you always wanted?"

"I must go where the work is, that's why I'm going. It cannot be helped, just for work."

Minami paused thoughtfully. "Please enjoy the obento salmon. Remember, Tokyo taste is weak for Tohoku people."

He smoothed his hair with a stern expression, appeasing an unruly tuft. Minami had thought it cute when his hair stood on end like this, but Shimoyama hated the cowlick, aware that behind his back some of his students had nicknamed him porcupine. As the part fell in line at last and he turned from the empty train to the darkness behind the window, his features became relaxed, his mouth less severe.

He was thinking of the woman in Ueno, the service that he desired.

They didn't mind just talking, a man at his school had said. They didn't care how you spent the time and would answer anything you asked, about women and how they were thinking and how you could tell if they loved you or not. Anything you were eager to know, as long as you paid for their time and showed them a little respect.

Minami loved trips, any travel. The more removed she was from Japan, the more at home, the more comfortable she seemed with herself. Back at home, she soon became small, afraid of challenging growth and escaping into little safe spaces. Instead of finding fulfillment in work or the idea of having a child, she had looked for exploits in the world, the callings of strange enchantment. She had traveled all over Asia, a backpacker on a shoestring budget moving by railroad through Mongolia and Myanmar, places all but unknown to Shimoyama. He was focused on life in Japan and not eager to travel much more, yet some of her stories had made him uneasy about foreign roads she had roamed, free in a way he had never been. An album showed her in Mongolia, a smile on her sunburned face, next to a short, dark man with no shirt, an unmade bed in the back. Shimoyama obsessed forever over what might have happened that night. Had she given herself to a stranger, a man who could never know her? A secret position she wouldn't have tried in her marriage?

The adventures that still flowed through her, the mystery of her travels and the life she had lived before him, were a part of who she became. A part of what kept them separate, a part of what had intrigued him.

"She will adore you," Ando had gushed at the wedding, his face flushed from too much sake. "She just won't let it show. Not ever."

Winter was milder in Tokyo than up north. At the bustling Ueno station, the gateway to the Tohoku region, most hats in the streets were a Santa Claus red, worn by the staff of convenience stores that offered discounted Christmas cakes. Some snow remained in the shade of the avenues, where it had frozen to cubist sculptures that dripped in the morning sun.

He was lost in no time, as though in another world. Doubt overcame him the moment he left the station, not sure where to go and embarrassed to ask for directions. In the maze of the pleasure district, men with small narrow eyes were moving along, hands in their pockets and faces solemn as doorways buzzed them inside, a secret known to them only. The signs on buildings climbed floor after floor in a gridlock of plastic and neon, marking soaplands and shot bars and bars with exotic hostesses. The sheer number of offerings overwhelmed, a casbah of carnal expenditure that needed a special map.

"First time around? We have special massage relaxation."

Shimoyama hastened his steps, away from the man in a trench coat. He knew the offerings, the list of specials, they weren't why he had come. He was here to talk to a woman and ask her about his wife, to get answers on what it meant when she acted the way she did. A hostess club was expensive and they kept conversations safe, to make men feel good and keep ordering overpriced drinks. His aim was different, however. He was here to unpack, to get to the bottom of things.

He slummed through the neon for more than an hour in ebbing hopes of being approached, his trolley creaking behind him as he searched for eyes to meet his. No woman stepped out of the shadows or the marque of a pachinko parlor, no one called in hushed tones and approached with a proposition. It can't be this hard, Shimoyama thought with growing despair, remembering the fellow teacher who had told him about Ueno. *I have money for this. I can pay.*

Minami sat in a small café, absorbed in a book before her. As she thoughtfully turned a page and smoothed it with her long fingers, her face shimmered in the sheen of a lamp. As always, she was alone, in the depths of her inner life.

So strange she now kept appearing, when in years of marriage he had chased her. A cloud insubstantial, afraid to be known. She couldn't have been more mysterious had she never spoken at all.

Some people said that Japanese women made good wives for men of the mind. They left you alone with your thoughts and respected intellectual work, as long as it paid the bills. Minami, however, was different. He often felt as if she weren't with him, not really there as they shared their meals or went out for a stroll in the hills, not even nights when they lay in bed. They were like spies sleeping next to each other, guarding their personal secrets.

The wish to be close, to get through her shell and see the secrets she kept inside, to learn her thoughts and her hidden needs—this wish had absorbed and vexed him. It shouldn't matter, he always thought, that she came from another culture. He had set out to crack the codes as though accepting a personal challenge, learning her language and Japanese manners with astounding devotion and care. However, Minami seemed unimpressed. She showed her gratitude not with words but repaid him with acts of service, which her husband had not understood as the language of love it was. Until the end, she had kept him guessing and made him try harder and harder, always hoping to catch a glimpse of the person she was inside. Like a squirrel hoarding nuts for the winter, she had received his attention and efforts, the tokens of how much he cared, then seemed to forget where she stashed them.

As she sat in the small café, a spot had shown on the upholstery. The stain had seeped through her dress into the mauve velour of the seat, darkening it by a shade.

Shimoyama looked down, his eyes full of shock. Then he turned and rushed back down the alley, past the standing bars and the noise and the shops with their curtained entrance, the smell of grilled pork in the air. He had to return to the neon, away from the awful stain and everything else that was now the past.

"From up north?" asked the hotel manager, a young man in a polyester suit, most likely a student on a part-time job. His oval face was clean-shaven, his hair moussed into a ducktail.

"Yamamoto. Near Sendai."

In the awkward silence that still followed mention of Sendai, not to mention the shock of a White man speaking fluently in Japanese, Shimoyama took in the lobby. Beside a shelf with stacks of used manga was a large pot with three bamboo shoots, adorned with flowers and bound together with straw, that ushered in the new year. A row of slippers lined on the tatami, pointing in the same direction.

"The area around the station . . ." Shimoyama began awkwardly. "A bit sketchy, it seems."

"I'm sorry?"

"Maybe not safe there, alone at night."

The manager looked up, comprehending. "I don't go for that business, never have. I see it but wouldn't pay for it."

Less business for you, Shimoyama thought grimly. He thanked the manager and said goodnight.

As he shuffled the silent corridors lined with capsules and personal lockers, he had a strange sense of coming home, like a sailor in a submarine moving deep underneath the sea. The pods were all taken, curtains drawn behind oval windows, except one at the end of the hall. From around a corner came the clanking of coins in a vending machine. A metal can, a highball or mixed nuts and crackers, tumbled down with a thump.

The air smelled like seaweed and brine, the deepest bowels of the ocean. A wave had eclipsed the sun and kept rising a towering black, till he dipped at the final moment and the mass washed over his head. He lost up and down as the water engulfed, then spun him around like a washing machine. He flailed in a horror of moments, unable to see the sky, the path that would let him breathe, then resurfaced, gasping for air. Another wave started mounting in the distance, foam on the rising crest, when he noticed the manager of the hotel, rather close in the sea beside him, soaked in his suit as if coming from work. He clutched a plank and was treading water when Shimoyama called out, "Have you seen my wife?"

The man stared at him, one elbow propped on the plank, then pointed to a house painted white that stood on a sandbank with dreamy assurance.

"Over there, at the clubhouse." A wave lifted him, then he was gone.

It was the phone ringing, not the tremors of another quake, that tore Shimoyama out of the dream. Alone in the capsule, the sheets stuffed around his feet, he felt feverishly in the dark for any wetness or tendrils of seaweed, until he made out the glimmer of the console, the television set in the wall. The screen of his phone, perched on a stack of samurai manga, showed the call as "ID unsent."

Fear moved down his spine, like a touch clammy from the sea. Raising himself on the futon, he stared at the phone display. The call was missed, impossible to return.

The supernatural became eerie in Tokyo, as if the towers man made of steel and the science that tamed darkness with neon insisted that it was impossible, that certain things shouldn't be. He was shocked that Minami had followed him, a possible wrench in his plans and a sign that his mind was unsound. Not here, he thought darkly. Not here and not now.

He curled up in the sheets, unaware of the smell of linoleum or the hum of the vending machine, the snores from the other capsules or the drunkenly shifting bodies returned from the year-end parties. He thought that the space was perfect, the most comfortable way to exist. He was safe from the reach of the ocean, and everything he needed was here.

Many people had seen dead loved ones, the ones who were lost to the sea and unable to move to heaven. They were chained to this world as shapes, roaming the coastline and villages for indefinite spells of time, their faces away from the shore as they passed without any greeting. They might even come to a house, sitting down at a table for tea and then dripping onto the tatami, eyes silently fixed on their cake. Some encounters were so disturbing that people asked priests for an exorcism. Most apparitions, however, were met with a matter-of-factness, an embrace of the supernatural that was common in parts of Tohoku. The winters were long and hard, and people spent nights sharing tales of the ghosts they had seen, invariably women who haunted the men responsible for their earthly unhappiness.

And wasn't it just like Minami? To emerge from the depths of the sea and then ask, did you miss me? To see how much he cared, see the look on his face and then leave. She seemed comfortable with herself, more or less. She just couldn't fathom how someone might love her, certainly not her own husband. She enjoyed separations and solitude, the times when he visited family or left for days on a teacher conference, as though it were easier to love him from a distance, to miss him when he wasn't there.

The first reunion was sweet. On the seashore in late autumn, he stood in front of a makeshift shrine assembled there after the earthquake. Some had left offerings for the missing at a small wooden altar: a bottle of sake from Fukushima, some notes and fruit and origami cranes. Shimoyama had brought mandarins from a market, the sort Minami enjoyed for dessert, and arranged them on the snowy stones. At some point, somehow sensing another presence, he opened his eyes and there she was standing beside him, face quiet, her hands folded behind her back. She must have been there for a while, watching the tears on his cheek.

"Mandarins, small and sweet . . ." Her voice was a murmur. "They look nice in the snow. Like in the story by Akutagawa."

It was a thing Minami would say, a thing only she would see. A smile showed on her oval face as she picked a mandarin from the altar and started peeling it with awkward fingers, the tangy aroma joining the smell of the sea.

A magical dusk enveloped them as Shimoyama watched the mandarin peel, the way it landed in the snow like flowers. When Minami had finished and the mandarin was unpeeled, her hand opened with absent slowness, dropping the fruit on the ground.

There were questions, so many things he wanted to know that he relished the chance to see her. But as Minami continued to appear, always wearing the same old slippers, the same faded housedress, and then as gradually, shyly, they started to talk, she wouldn't share with him any thoughts or feelings, never mentioned their life together. She gave no sign of anguish or loss, nor was there anything she seemed to want. She never said what had happened since the tsunami, where she came from or where she went. It was all weather and food and small things, the same evasion, the same stubborn refusal to let him close. No deeper exchange or conversation, no confession of love at last. He was foiled again, at a loss. A man starved to make a connection with a maddeningly private ghost.

A week before the tsunami, Minami came home from a doctor appointment, undone by a test result. A shadowy speck in her breast, calling for further tests. Shimoyama couldn't believe it. Her breasts were so small, like persimmons, how could they harbor a tumor?

He said not to worry, a false alarm, then embraced her like a long-stemmed vase. She was silent in his absent arms, listening not to the words, which she knew couldn't help, but the presence of his embrace. Her cheek on his sweater, she stood waiting for his arms to slacken, the warmth of his body to leave. It was he who ended their hugs, his choice to let go, every time, and then later Shimoyama wondered if perhaps she had wanted more. Had he stayed for another moment and waited for her to stir, had the embrace, just once, concluded at her own pace, would that have been time that she needed?

Minami was scared of dying, because she desperately wanted to live and keep doing the things she liked doing, like studying aromatherapy and learning about new smells. She couldn't handle her vulnerability, her loss of control in the relationship. For the first time since he had known her, the oval face showed her age, marked with fear.

She was scared of dying and then she died, alone in a wave that closed on a mystery. And now she shows up just to say hello and I don't know what to do with her.

Sometimes he wished she would stop appearing and allow him a little closure, a little peace, no longer making him fear for his mind.

He did not have the heart to tell her that she was dead.

The city held endless distraction, a mass of people that overwhelmed. Unlike the lumbering shells of Yamamoto, the people here rushed as though arrival had meaning, as though each delay were of consequence as they nodded into their phones. Shimoyama adored the lights, the shops and the things that they sold, the purpose it all implied. Some people complained that Tokyo received its light from Tohoku, that the countryside hosted the plants, unsightly and less safe than promised, that made power for the large cities. As long as he could remember, Tohoku had been impoverished and sent labor and resources to the capital, yet in spite of the accident at the plant, Shimoyama felt no injustice. He roamed around, eyes wide and awed, filled with pride in his adopted country as he gazed at neon displays, the endlessly flashing stars that made up the heart of Shinjuku. If Tohoku could assist the splendor, it would be an honor to do so.

He lunched at a shop every day, salting his soba and slurping in a show of relish. He took trains to see where they went, the Ginza and Tozai and Marunouchi, like sighs deep inside the behemoth. Having reached the end of a line, he would walk around a few steps, then sit down in a station café with a cup of coffee and a sandwich. Most guests were men reading newspapers and books and Shimoyama was glad they were there, lingering until the place closed. He liked Japanese men who worked hard and enjoyed their own time alone. He liked the musty smell of their suits, the way they smoked through their packs until it was time to go home.

On the night train, everybody desired. Women asleep like dolls in a dream, as beautiful as escape. He looked at them for a moment, then closed his eyes in the crowd and savored the face in his mind. In the press of silent humanity, he never stopped searching for eyes to meet his, the agreement on a transaction. His money lasted for a few more days. After that, there were no more plans.

"I'm interested." He pressed the phone to his ear. "When does it start? And what did you say were the hours?"

"Six to eight, the contract is ready." The man from the agency sounded eager. "Sundays off until further notice. We might need you as needs arise."

"Protective gear?"

"A suit and a mask, each night you get checked for exposure. The contract renews every week."

Shimoyama leaned back in his capsule, one arm under his head. The ads called for laborers in Fukushima, to help secure the nuclear power plants and build tanks for the contaminated water. The pay was minimum wage, no insurance, no questions about immigrant status.

"I'll be in touch."

He hung up and swung his legs into the capsule, then drew the curtain and sank onto the futon.

A mild sun had appeared outside, and for a while, he just lay there and listened to the icicles, a soft patter against the wall. He knew the recruiter hadn't been honest, the way the government and the media weren't honest, about contamination and risk of exposure around the plants and the nearby areas. He wouldn't call back, convinced the recruiter was a front for the mob. He was scared of the radiation and needs they said might arise, the amulet round his neck spelling death in a creaking code.

A mantle of snow lay over the park, the wide stone steps at the southern entrance and the statue of Saigo Takamori, a samurai in green bronze with a dog on a short leash. A veil of ice filmed his head and the hand resting on his sword, like a patina of the Satsuma rebellion. Saigo had died the death of a samurai after fighting the Kagoshima government, beheaded by a warrior comrade when the final battle was lost.

Shimoyama stood near the station, shuddering in the cold while his eyes kept scanning the street. A gentle snow fell like dreams. The city lay under enchantment, its vast endless hustle a snowscape of calm. The neon was at last shut off, allowing a magical stillness all the way to the Marui department store.

"Are you eating well?" Minami looked worried. "Any news about work?"

She wore a woolen scarf with the housedress and seemed unmoved by the cold. Behind her loomed the office towers, dark and empty with the solemn emptiness that marks the end of the year.

"Take good care of yourself and eat well. They have rice bowls and eel at Ameyoko. You should try it, you like eel so much."

Her breath didn't steam as she spoke. Her fingers clutched the hem of the dress, which was spattered with crusted mud.

"How does it matter so much, Samu-chan? Why did you come all the way just for this?"

He was silent, the tables turned, as Minami rushed into speech.

"The poor things, they are from the countryside. The yakuza take their papers, then force them to pay off a debt. They don't want to do this, not at all. It is better if you don't go. You shouldn't go, Samu-chan. It's not right!"

His anger, buried for years, welled up like mud in the ocean. A stubbornness all his own filled his heart.

"Your hair . . ." With the odd fake laugh that he hated, she raised a hand to smooth the stray tuft. "It looks funny, like a little pointer. Just a moment."

He ached to take her by the shoulders, but then the words came. "You're not here, not really. I understand that."

"What do you mean?" She looked shocked.

"You are not here, and I am alone. Can you not see that?"

It was the most hurtful thing he had ever said, certainly to his wife. He turned away, his face ashen, then stumbled off to the gate that led deeper into the park. The passersby were indifferent, observing the scene without judgment.

Through the unfeeling cold and the snowflakes blundering through the dark, he heard slippers flapping behind him. The fading sound mixed with the swish of the housedress and a soft plaintive cry that came from a place far away.

"Samu-chan, stay! Please don't go! Samu-chan, please!"

The space was partitioned by drapes, vague in the dimmed red light. On the wall hung a cheap faded painting, yellow roses in tumescent full bloom.

He had returned from the shower and toweled off, finding his clothes on a chair, the sole furniture in the room besides an old narrow cot. A smell of baby oil hovered nearby, and when the woman pushed through the drapes and approached him with dreamy assurance, the voice of another woman, a surreptitious sliding of doors, came from behind the partition.

The man in the trench coat had greeted him at the door, relieved to see that Shimoyama spoke Japanese. His manner was all discreet as he asked for payment up front, then he handed Shimoyama a towel and a straw basket for his clothes. Steering him down a hallway, the man pointed to a small bathroom, a shower stall without a curtain. Shimoyama went in, then locked the low door behind him.

Rushing aimlessly through Ueno, still upset from the scene in the park, he had run into the man again. The same call, the same offering, but this time Shimoyama stopped. He had abandoned his plan, no more need to see his wife explained or find out if she ever loved him. There was something in the approach, though, the sound of massage relaxation and on top they had New Year discounts, that spoke to him in his rage.

Stretched out on the threadbare cot, a towel on his naked loins, another one under his head, he looked at the woman in a yukata. He wasn't sure if he found her attractive—coarse hair falling on her shoulders, the lined features and sagging cheeks with the makeup of middle age—and yet somehow this urged his arousal.

"From up north, *onii-san*? I thought you are from America."

"Yamamoto, near Sendai."

She looked down on him, her teeth uneven. "I once visited there," she said in broken Japanese. "The ramen was good, a bit salty. Forgive my rudeness, onii-san."

She removed the small towel that covered him, then, taking a bottle of oil from the chair, squeezed an ample amount on her palm. The oil was warm on his skin as with sure studied moves, she started listlessly kneading his legs. Shimoyama knew the massage was for sake of appearance, a legal front for her trade. Her hands skirted the place where the shadows were deepest, but then, abruptly, she stopped.

"You want stronger than this, onii-san?"

The roses on the wall became blurred, the yellow fraught with eternity. A deep breath, his eyes nodding yes. He glanced at her sandaled feet.

"You have money? It's not cheap, onii-san . . ."

She took the jacket and fished out his wallet, extracting the bills that mattered, then kept rummaging through the wallet and took out the rest of the bills. She shook the coins out and stuffed them into her pocket, then, seeing his watch on the chair, gave him a look that questioned. Surprised by the ask, Shimoyama made no response and the watch joined the cash in her pocket. The woman looked down and away, then patted his arm.

"Be back in a flash."

He had lain on the sheet for a while and was starting to feel absurd, wondering if he should call or look for the man in the trench coat, when the drapes rustled sharply on the track. A mutter that sounded like an order, then from the edge of his vision he saw shapes stepping into the room, dressed in cheap dark suits, their hard faces set.

The car was empty, the train was local to Saitama. Every time the train shifted tracks or made one of its frequent stops, an old newspaper slipped down the aisle, the most notable sound in the car as it moved through the Tokyo suburbs.

The first day of the new year saw everyone home with their families, eating *osechi* from lacquered boxes and drinking sake from early morning. People stepped out into the cold to wait in long lines at a shrine, where they bought fortunes and charms and then prayed for health and prosperity. It was slow, the slowest day of the year, a whole-island standstill. A day of family meetings and extended meals, of watching variety shows on TV and letting time pass by without thought. A day that was long for those who greeted the new year alone.

Shimoyama planned to arrive early, in part because he was out of money. A couple of telephone interviews and he was hired as a substitute teacher at a junior high school in Misato. The school needed teachers, and quick, and while Shimoyama preferred to teach high school, he had agreed without second thought.

Minami sat across the aisle, her gaze on the setting sun. The housedress was dry and neat, as though she had managed to get it cleaned and pressed. She looked ready to meet family for *oshogatsu*, or perhaps leave for one of her trips to a place far away.

No answer when he asked if she was cold or if she wanted the tsukemono from his lunch, the salmon he bought at the station. He made a show of checking the bandage, the spot on his nose where a blow had landed as the men threw him out of the room, to tempt Minami to come and check. However, she stayed in her seat. She likely had the wrong idea about what happened at the massage, which, anyway, was hard to explain. She would acknowledge him sooner or later, he just had to wait for a chance. For a while he just sat there, hands in his pockets, thinking about what lay ahead.

A bell clanged monotonously in the dark, then faded away in the distance. The train rattled past a gate, abandoned in neon. As if on a cue, Shimoyama rose and then crossed down the aisle, sitting down next to his wife. The seat was heated and soft and he was careful not to touch her side, leaning back with a feigned indifference, the way he used to when she was mad.

Minami gazed out the window, unmoved as the pane shook briefly in the draft. An elbow on the wooden sill, she was resting her head on her hand, the fingers on her soft pale cheek. Her eyes dreamed in the changing landscape, the towns and occasional plains with their white winter trees, the fields soon to be worked by the farmers.

www.ingramcontent.com/pod-product-compliance
Lightning Source LLC
LaVergne TN
LVHW041940070526
838199LV00051BA/2849